◆ ◆ ◆

I am sitting on the bleachers by the middle school baseball diamond watching four guys play catch. They're actually pretty good. Two of them were in my science class.

The tall, skinny guy has a good arm, throwing fast to the shortest guy, who jumps up to catch it and doesn't miss. He turns around fast and throws it to an African American kid, who scoops it up and shouts, "Wake up, Lopez!" and throws it long to the fourth guy, who says, "I'm awake, Terrell!" and blasts it back.

The good news: these guys have accuracy and hustle—two big pluses in serious baseball.

The not-so-good news: there are only four of them. You need nine players for a team, plus a few extra.

OTHER BOOKS YOU MAY ENJOY

SOAR

JOAN BAUER

SOAR

PUFFIN BOOKS

PUFFIN BOOKS
An imprint of Penguin Random House LLC
375 Hudson Street
New York, New York 10014

First published in the United States of America by Viking,
an imprint of Penguin Random House LLC, 2016
Published by Puffin Books, an imprint of Penguin Random House LLC, 2017

THE LIBRARY OF CONGRESS HAS CATALOGED THE VIKING EDITON AS FOLLOWS:
Bauer, Joan.
Soar / Joan Bauer
pages cm
ISBN 9780451470348 (hardcover)
Summary: Moving to Hillcrest, Ohio, when his adoptive father accepts a temporary job, twelve-
year-old Jeremiah, a heart transplant recipient, has sixty days to find a baseball team to coach.
[1. Moving, Household—Fiction. 2. Heart—Transplantation—Fiction. 3. Baseball—Fiction.
4. Coaches (Athletics)—Fiction. 5. Teamwork (Sports)—Fiction. 6. Adoption—Fiction.]
I. Title.
PZ7.B32615So 2016 [Fic]—dc23 2015013293

Puffin Books ISBN 9780147513151

Printed in the United States of America

Book design by Nancy Brennan

10

For Evan and Jean, one of the first father/daughter duos to attend the Father & Son Baseball Camp in Cooperstown.

Chapter

1

I'M PROBABLY TWELVE years old; that's what the doctors think. I could have been born anywhere, but it was most likely in Indianapolis, Indiana—at least that's where I've decided I was born, because that's where I was found. Specifically, I was found at Computer Partners Ltd. in the snack room, right by the coffeepot. I think it's one of the reasons that I like the taste of coffee—it reminds me of home. I was found by Walt Lopper, a computer geek who had never so much as diapered a baby, but there I was, and I'm told it was clear that I did need a new diaper. I needed a lot of other things, too, but my bottle wasn't empty, so the police felt that meant I hadn't been there long. Walt found me at seven a.m. on October third—it was his turn to make coffee and he always got to work early. I was in my baby chair with a note:

pleez tek car of him Bcaz he my best boy
I no yur good!

There weren't any other clues about who left me there, but I'm inclined to believe it was my mother, who might have worked nights cleaning office buildings. I had a little stuffed eagle that I was gnawing on, but other than that it was your usual thing. Walt called the police and they came and took me to the station and then someone from child services came and took me to a safe place, although Computer Partners Ltd. was a safe place, real safe, otherwise my mother wouldn't have left me there. I'm told I didn't cry, I just watched people and took things in, but if you wanted to see what I was made of, try taking the stuffed eagle from my little hands. I'd yank it back and screech, "No!"

They think I was nine months old when I was found, so saying "no" is a pretty big deal. Walt says it indicates I had a big brain, possibly like Einstein. Walt has a big brain. He's officially a computer genius, but even bigger than his brain is his heart, which he says he hadn't paid that much attention to until I came along.

The police tried to find the person who left me. I refuse to use the word *abandoned* because I'm fairly certain that my mother loved me and didn't have much choice but to leave me. I'm also fairly certain that she knew it was Walt's day to make the coffee. I think she probably checked out who was in that company and would never have left me there on a Monday, which was Dirk Dagwood's day to make coffee. From what I've heard, he might not even have noticed a baby sitting there chewing on a stuffed eagle. He was that kind of clueless.

It took a while for Walt to adopt me, being a single man and all. He had to get trained and certified as a foster parent. It took another year of my living with him to convince the judge he should be my official dad. Walt spent a lot of time trying to figure me out, and I'm told he talked to me like I was a baby genius. He read me articles from computer magazines, he took computers apart and told me what he was doing and why. During baseball season we watched the games together and he told me how the pitcher was trying to psych out the batter and what some of the signals meant. My favorite signal involved tapping your nose, which Walt said could mean anything, depending on the day. I tapped my nose a lot, and Walt carried me around explaining what everything was and how the world was a pretty complicated place, which I already knew.

When the adoption went through, Walt said, "It's official now. Okay?"

"Okay," I said. After that I started talking to Walt and to my stuffed eagle that I named Baby. I didn't talk to anyone else until later.

The problem with having a story like this is people don't know what to do with it. Their faces get super sad and their shoulders slump as they pat me on the head, which I find irritating, and say, "My, you are a little survivor, aren't you?"

Well, I suppose I am. But since I don't remember the first few years of my life, I don't feel like I can take any credit for it. And then there's the issue of my birthday, which is a theory, but schools seem to need an actual date, so I count three months ahead from October third when I was found to early January. I give the doctor a fudge factor in his estimate of one week, which puts my birthday on January tenth. Getting close is important to me.

I've lived in four different places, because Walt is a consultant and has to move around a lot. At my last two schools my class was learning the recorder. I'm so done with this instrument. I can play "Go Tell Aunt Rhody" in my sleep. I told Eddie Bartok, who was failing recorder, to pretend he was a snake charmer—they play instruments like this and get the snakes to dance to the music. This caused Eddie to practice like crazy, but his mother wouldn't get him a snake. He tried charming worms in the garden, but worms today, they couldn't care less. He played "Go Tell Aunt Rhody" to his dog, who yelped and ran away. Once Eddie was at my house with his recorder and he tried to charm Baby.

"Inanimate things don't respond!" I mentioned.

And anyway, nobody can charm an eagle.

You can't keep an eagle in a cage or have one for a pet.

The number one rule for eagles is they have to be free.

I'm sure this is why my mother gave me that stuffy. She knew I had an eagle inside of me. Not everybody does.

But when you do, you'd better pay attention and deal with it, because if you don't, you'll have one intensely frustrating life.

Chapter

2

"I HAVE A new consulting gig," Walt tells me. "They pay up front."

This is excellent news, because lots of Walt's clients take forever to pay him. Walt has his own consulting company, the Magellan Group. It's not a group, exactly, and no one is named Magellan; it's named after Ferdinand Magellan, our favorite dead-for-centuries explorer, who, like Walt, worked 24/7.

"Where is it?" I ask.

"Ohio."

We're living in St. Louis and I really, really like it here.

"They need me for a couple of months, Jer. It's kind of an emergency."

Everything Walt does is somebody's emergency. No

one calls my father and says, "Hey, all systems are go here. Just wanted you to know."

"Where in Ohio?" I ask.

"Near Cincinnati, but I don't think—"

"The Cincinnati Reds are looking strong this year, Walt." They're my third favorite team.

"They are, but I don't think—"

"The name of the town, Walt . . ."

"A smaller place than Cincinnati. Hillcrest, Ohio."

"They have a hill with a crest, right?"

Walt laughs. "Maybe. They have a company there and . . ."

The "and" part is always "and they need a little help." Believe me, when Walt Lopper gets called in, it's because people need a lot of help.

"They've got a little problem, Jer."

"What kind of problem?"

"Their robots keep falling down."

"Why?"

"It's unclear."

I look in the corner. "Jerwal, are you awake?"

Jerwal, the robot Walt and I built together, glows and beeps.

Walt hasn't thought about taking any out-of-town business for a long time, because of my heart. Four years ago, I had a perfectly healthy heart. Then something called cardiomyopathy happened and everything changed.

I look at Walt, who sat with me every day I was in the hospital, who never once made me feel like I wasn't his kid, or was any kind of disappointment or a drain on his life.

"When do you have to be there?"

"Yesterday, Jer."

Today is March twenty-seventh, and lots is about to happen here.

The Cardinals' opening day is April thirteenth and we have tickets.

The science fair at my school is coming up and I've been working on a project that shows the trajectory of a well-hit baseball in 3-D. I've been thinking about contacting the manager of the St. Louis Cardinals to come see it—my findings could be big.

I take a deep breath and pull out my phone. Research is critical to decision making.

"Hillcrest, Ohio," I read to him. "Population 12,761,

located in Ohio's rich farmland in the western part of the state. A small Midwestern town known for the excellence of its high school baseball program." This is getting interesting. "The Hillcrest High School Hornets have won six state championships and twice clinched the nationals." I look up. "We can gorge ourselves on baseball, Walt!"

Walt's face has that half-sunk look it gets when he hasn't told me everything.

"I think, Jer . . . Well . . . I called your aunt Charity—"

"No."

"Let me finish. I called her and she said she would stay here with you so you could finish school and—"

"No!"

"I want you to stay near Dr. Feinberg."

"There are doctors in Cincinnati."

"Wonderful doctors, no doubt."

"Do you care about my heart, Walt?"

"What kind of a question is that?"

An unfair question.

"She treats me like I'm a little kid!"

"I think if we talk to her—"

"We've done that. Aunt Charity smothers me." I

feel my face get hot. "She makes me wash my hands hundreds of times."

"You are supposed to avoid infection, my man."

"Walt, please. I don't need to be a fanatic about it." I squirt antiseptic goo on my hands and rub it in, counting to ten. "She asks me every morning"—I can hardly say it—"if I've had a bowel movement!"

"That's a tough one, Jer, but we do need to make sure all systems are go." He laughs at his joke.

"And do I have to even mention that she forced me against my will to make angel ornaments with little puffy skirts?"

Walt shakes his head. "I know. But she's been here for us. She's really helped out."

Aunt Charity stayed with us for eight months when I was in and out of the hospital. I'm totally grateful she did this.

"She's my only sister. What can I tell you?"

"You can tell me she's not coming and I can go with you. I love her, okay? I just can't live with her right now." Or possibly ever.

Walt stands up. "It's only for a couple of months. What could happen?"

Phone again. I look up "shortest wars in history."

There's lots of material here. "Whole wars have been fought in less than thirty days, Walt. Can you really take the chance?"

Walt sips his coffee and looks at the map of the ancient world that I gave him for his birthday. It shows how wrong they were back in the 1500s. This was what Magellan had to deal with. Despite all that, he circumnavigated the globe before people knew it was a globe.

Is that vision or what?

"You're telling me, Jer, you want to leave sixth grade at the end of March and come with me to Hillcrest, Ohio, where I will be working day and night?"

I nod.

"What would you be doing there?" Walt persists.

"Gaining brilliance?"

"You're already too smart."

"I'd go to school and I'd help you. I could make dinner and—"

Walt shakes his head. His beard is getting some gray in it. People say it makes him look distinguished. He's wearing the T-shirt I got him for Father's Day—it has a mug of coffee and, underneath that, the words GAME CHANGER.

It's kind of our story.

"Jerwal," I say, "come forward." Jerwal moves slowly toward us. "Would you like to help the robots who are falling down?"

Jerwal has no idea, but he likes hearing his name. It took us months to get the voice-activated part working. We had to shorten his name because he couldn't understand "Jerwalthian," as in *The Jerwalthian has entered the atmosphere.*

Walt sips more coffee. "I'm sorry about how I live. I want you to have a stable environment."

"I don't feel unstable, Walt."

"You know what I mean. Not so much change."

"You don't change."

He laughs. "You're referring to my wardrobe?"

Walt wears blue shirts with jeans or khakis most days.

I stretch out my arms like I'm flying. "So we just swoop into Hillcrest and make it happen."

Walt sips coffee, thinking.

I sip decaf. "Jerwal, do you want to go play with the robots in Ohio?" Jerwal beeps and moves his head and arms from side to side.

Walt points a finger of ultimate authority at me. "For me to even consider it, Jer—and I'm not saying I am—Dr. Feinberg needs to sign off on this one hundred percent. You understand that might not happen."

I clear my throat. "I understand that in any contest, I will be tested, maybe to the boundaries of my ability. And when this happens, I will remember that I have overcome great difficulties already, and all that strength is in me."

Walt sniffs. "Which coach said that?"

"I just created it."

"Not bad."

When I'm a coach I'm going to tell my players to say that. I write it down.

Walt studies my face.

"I'm fine, Walt."

I say that a lot because it's true.

It's got to be true.

Chapter 3

NOT EVERYONE ON my transplant team could be here. We got this appointment fast.

Dr. Curchink is out sick and Dr. Meredith has an emergency with another patient, but Dr. Feinberg is here, and Hassan the transplant nurse, and Millard the tech guy, who keeps track of everything. Millard just gave me an echocardiogram to test the strength of my heart with sound waves. Hassan gets a blood sample from my left arm. I make a fist.

"Your blood's still red," Hassan says.

"I've been working hard to keep it red," I tell him.

Hassan smiles.

There's a plastic heart on the counter. So many people just take their hearts for granted. I did until third grade, when I caught a virus that slowly began attacking my heart muscle. I got a lot of colds that year. I wasn't eating much. I'd run and have trouble breathing. We thought it was asthma at first. It wasn't even close to that.

Being a computer genius, Walt knew about viruses. "We're going to find out what's going on with you," he told me. "That's going to mean a lot of tests, and probably a few extra doctors."

"I don't want extra doctors."

You don't always get what you want.

Two years later, I had to have a heart transplant. I was ten. I don't recommend the experience, but I can promise you, it's so much better than dying.

I told Aunt Charity I wanted to keep my old heart in a jar at home to remember, but she started screaming about the intense grossness of that.

"I made it to ten years of age with that heart," I told her. "It's part of me."

She threw up her hands and said absolutely not.

"He's kidding about keeping it at home," Walt assured her.

We gave it to science—the best solution—although first I wanted to use it for the science fair at school.

"How can you even think of these things?" she shrieked.

"Maybe we can visit it?" I asked her.

That didn't work, either.

Right now Dr. Feinberg, who did my transplant surgery, is looking at me like he always does—checking my eyes without saying he is, checking to see if I have energy without saying he is.

Walt says, "We want zero risk, doctor. We are open to whatever you think is best."

"Which would be me going to Ohio."

Dr. Feinberg is looking at my test results. "Jeremiah, as long as I have known you, you've always been clear as to what you want. How are you feeling?"

"Fine. Really fine."

"How's the energy level?"

"You know, it's okay."

A medical nod. "Arrhythmia? Swollen ankles? Brain fog? Nausea? An uncontrollable desire to play meaningless, soul-crushing video games all day?"

"Only the last one."

"Shortness of breath?"

I breathe like it's hard.

Dr. Feinberg looks at me. "This is a joke?"

"Yes."

"You'll be gone how long?"

Walt says, "Two months or so. But if this isn't a good idea—"

"That's a lot of compacted stress: packing, saying good-bye, moving, a new school, and then coming back."

Walt says, "If you don't think this is a good idea—"

"I want to understand," Dr. Feinberg adds. He always says this. It's why he's a great doctor.

Walt starts explaining about this new consulting gig he's got, but he's not selling the concept. He hasn't once mentioned the stress of living with Aunt Charity. He has hardly touched on the theme of baseball and how tomorrow's stars are playing on the Hillcrest Hornets today, how it's a chance to see them before they get really big, how their champion pitcher throws an unbelievable fastball.

I interrupt and make my case. I also emphasize the robots.

"How fast does the kid throw?" Dr. Feinberg asks.

"Ninety-four miles per hour."

Millard, Hassan, and Dr. Feinberg nod, impressed.

I say, "This is a once-in-a-lifetime opportunity."

That's a big sentence for me. Before I got my new heart, I was so sick, I wasn't going to make it. That surgery went pretty well, considering where I was starting from. They hoped it would have gone a little better.

My scar from the transplant runs from the top of my chest to the middle. I showed it to my best friend, Yaff, who said, "Tell people you got attacked by zombies and survived."

I can walk blocks at a time, but I still can't run.

"Jeremiah," Dr. Feinberg says, "you need to be aware of two things. First, you will need to have another team in Ohio and check in with them."

I know this.

"Second, you have to be uniquely careful of infection."

The team stares at me. I say I know that, too.

"We are talking about bathing in antiseptic lotion."

I take out the bottle from my pocket.

"We are talking about naps."

I groan.

"And you must have realistic goals for your time there. Do you have those?"

"I want to see as many baseball games as I can, and I want to do well in school and hang out with Walt and maybe build another robot."

They are still staring at me like that's not enough.

"Okay, and I will run away screaming if I see anyone sneezing."

"No running," the doctor says.

I nod. I hate the no running part. I tried running after my surgery and that didn't go too well.

"And I won't eat at salad bars because of the germs."

"They're infested with germs," Hassan reminds me.

"And when I'm at baseball games, if I feel tired or anything, I will let Walt know."

Still staring.

"It's what I do here!"

"We'll discuss this and be back in a few minutes." Dr. Feinberg walks toward the door with the team.

"Don't forget the part you can't put on a chart," I shout. "Baseball and robots. How can this not be good for my heart?"

The doctor smiles. Millard doesn't. They walk out.

Walt says, "You know, whatever they decide, it's for the best."

I look at him. His eyes are kind, but tired.

I can do this, Walt!

The team comes back. I try to read their faces like people do on legal shows when the jury walks in to give the verdict.

I put my hand over my heart.

"We are unanimous in this, Jeremiah," Dr. Feinberg

begins. And the team stands tough behind him.

I think it's no.

"For baseball and robots and being with your dad, you can go to Ohio."

"Yes!" I shout.

"I want you to write this across your eyeballs, Jeremiah: do not take on too much."

"This is a great medical decision, you guys. You work together as a team and that's why you can get out there and make a difference."

Dr. Feinberg writes something down. "I will miss you, Jeremiah. I'm still hoping you can be the subject of the book that I will write someday when I have time to go on the talk show circuit."

The book is about the power of being hopeful and positive when you're a heart patient. He says I'm the poster boy for that.

"I'm referring you to a fine cardiologist I know in Cincinnati, Dr. Sarah Dugan. She was a resident here."

"If she's writing a book, I'll save the good stuff for you, Dr. F. I swear."

"Don't be stupid out there," Dr. Feinberg warns.

"I will be highly intelligent and totally aware at every moment."

"And don't forget to have fun."

"Yes, sir, I will do that!"

◆ ◆ ◆

Walt and I walk down the corridor and stop at the photos on the wall. The sign above them reads: OUR KIDS. These are the pictures of kids who had heart transplants here. There are baby pictures and pictures of people getting married. The point is, we get better and go on to have good lives. The one famous guy on the wall is Rodney P. Sears, who had three surgeries and now writes horror films about evil hearts that take over a person's body. His new movie is called *Heart of Stone: The Ever-Darkening Crevice*. Walt won't let me see it. There are three pictures of me, when I was eight, nine, and eleven. I look a lot better at eleven. I'd like to get on the board for doing something big—although surviving and getting strong is a nontrivial thing.

I'd like someone to point to my picture one day and say, "And now this young man is managing a major league baseball team."

Chapter
4

PACKING FOR THIS trip is the same as packing for life. I'm bringing too much, but I am easily bored. I pile up my forty-seven baseball and coaching books, which come up to my waist. They can fit in the trunk. I'm bringing my glove, my bat, my baseball.

Before my heart got that virus, Walt and I used to play catch every day, even in the winter—we painted a ball neon red so we could find it in the snow.

I'm all about dedication.

Yaff is sitting on the bed. "You're coming back, right?"

"In a couple of months."

Yaff looks unsure.

"All my doctors are here."

Yaff stretches out his leg. He got the first operation

to lengthen his leg last year. We met at the hospital in an elevator. We were both wearing Cardinals caps.

"It doesn't look like it, but my leg is growing," he said to me.

How can you not be friends with someone like that?

"I asked my mom if you could stay with us while your dad is in Ohio, Jeremiah. I told her you could train Powderpuff." That's Yaff's mother's extreme little white dog. "I told her this would change life in our family. My mom said if she had more strength and courage, you could."

"Thanks." Yaff's mother is a great mother role model. She always tells you how it is, and she gives you credit for understanding.

Time to pack the robot. "Jerwal, go to sleep."

Jerwal shuts down.

"My mom said Jerwal can stay with us, Jeremiah."

"He is needed elsewhere." I put Jerwal in a box, tuck a blanket around him for padding. Jerwal was a big friend of mine when I was in the hospital.

I hand Yaff a little card I printed. "Don't forget."

He turns it over, looks at it, and nods. "Yeah. I won't."

I don't give these cards to just anyone.

Yaff and I go back to watching the eagle cam from the Nature Conservancy. We are watching live-as-it-happens moments of two baby eagles in a nest as they deal with the unfairness of life. First, three days ago, their mother was killed. Now they're waiting for their father to come back with food.

Yaff shakes his head. "I don't think the father's coming back."

"Bet you he does." It's still hard to watch this.

"Loser cleans the winner's room."

This is an unfair bet because Yaff's room, according to his mother, has "the ambience of a Turkish prison."

The eagle cam is watched by so many people; it's been a big connect for me as an eagle watcher. I don't think my mother had any idea what she started when she got me that stuffy. I look over at Baby, who is in a plastic bag for safety. Her talons aren't what they used to be.

"Baby," I say, "what's your best guess on the father?"

Baby keeps things to herself, but now on the eagle cam, there's a swoosh of wings and the father swoops into the nest.

"Yes!" I shout.

People are commenting online:

It's another eagle!

It's a predator!!!!!!

I type, *This is what father eagles do, people* . . .

The father eagle has food for the babies, and he is patient. The baby eagles seem like challenged eaters, probably because of all the earlier trauma.

I win.

Yaff cleans my room like he cleans his room— badly. He shoves things in the closet and under the bed while I pack Baby. Yaff is the kind of friend who understands the power of historic stuffies. He still has Fiend, his king cobra stuffy. He wraps it around his neck on Halloween.

I'm going to need to find a good friend fast in Hillcrest.

I tape Baby's box shut. "Later, Baby," Yaff says.

I wish Yaff could come with me. He puts his arms out like wings. I do, too.

"See you in the summer, Eagle Man."

◆ ◆ ◆

"I think this is an unwise decision," Aunt Charity announces. "I am concerned on multiple levels." She drove over to say good-bye.

Walt hugs her. "We're going to give it a try."

"And if it's a disaster?" she demands.

I don't want to think about that!

He smiles kindly. "You'll be the first one to know, Char."

"Call the doctor first, then me." Aunt Charity hugs me and messes up my hair like I'm still eight years old.

We get in the car; she stands there waving until we turn the corner.

"I love her, Walt. I do."

"I know."

And we are off to live in Baseball Land . . .

◆　◆　◆

We are driving by the Gateway Arch—the tallest arch in the world. It's made of stainless steel and manages to glisten even on a cloudy day. We've been to the top of it four times. Every time I see it, I remember the early pioneers who pushed west to see what was beyond Missouri. That's what the arch is for—to help you think about courage.

Those people had strong hearts and vision.

My heart's not strong, but my vision makes up for it.

I take out my folder. On the cover I drew my signature mark, two curved lines coming together, like wings:

"I've been researching the high school team, Walt. The Hornets' star pitcher, Hargie Cantwell, has an ERA under two!"

That's earned run average. That means when this Hargie kid pitches seven innings, the other teams can only score one or two runs against him.

Walt was a pitcher in college. "That kid's got some heat."

"Last year the Hornets were undefeated."

"Impressive."

"They have a stadium. People call it the Hornets' Nest. And on this map"—I hold up a map of Hillcrest—

"it looks like the house we're renting is close to the stadium. How excellent is that?"

"I'm glad you're looking forward to it."

"There's a game today at four o'clock, Walt."

He drives a little faster. Three hundred and eleven miles to go.

We're on I–70 East in Illinois, zooming toward Indiana.

I remember when we moved from Indiana to St. Louis. We needed to be near Aunt Charity so she could help take care of me.

A lot of my time in St. Louis was spent in the hospital or at home. First, I got medication to make my heart pump better. But everything the doctors tried worked for a few months and then stopped. For two years I was in and out of the hospital; I could only go to school for part of the year. Aunt Charity and Walt tutored me. Walt is a cool tutor—we built our first robot (pre-Jerwal), we took a computer apart and put it back together, we built a radio. Aunt Charity made me write three-paragraph essays like "How Adversity Has Made Me Stronger" and "Why I Will Never Give Up." I tried a shortcut on the giving up one.

Why I Will Never Give Up
  by Jeremiah Lopper, Age 10

  I will never give up because I have too many
cool things to do to waste time being negative.

The End

Walt had that on the refrigerator for the longest time. Walt's uncle Jack (my great-uncle) laughed when he saw it. "Kid," he told me, "you're going places." I made a copy of it for him and he carried it in his wallet. He died last year when his heart gave out. Right before that he told me, "The best thing Walt ever did was bringing you into the family."

Two hundred and eighty-three miles to go.

"Are you up for more data, Walt?"

"Shoot."

"There are 12,761 people in Hillcrest, Ohio."

"Soon to be 12,763," he says.

"Right. The town motto is, and you're going to love

this, 'Life is a game. Baseball is serious.'"

Walt laughs. "I guess we know what they're about."

"Totally. They have two ice-cream shops and only one pizza place."

"Only one?"

"Junk Ball Pizza. It's near the stadium, which is only one-point-seven miles from our house. I can walk one-point-seven miles, Walt."

"Sometimes you can."

"Let's be positive."

Walt chuckles. "I found a hornets' nest once when I was a boy. That was not fun."

Lots more driving.

I've got questions:

Who will my friends be?

What are they doing right now?

Will they know right away that they need a new friend, or will I have to convince them?

"What do you think it's going to be like in Hillcrest, Walt?"

He smiles. "We'll know when we get there."

"I want to know before we get there."

"Takes the fun out of it, Jer."

Lots more driving.

Lots.

And then a huge baseball bat glistens on a little hill.

And after that, we see the ultimate sign:

TO THOSE WHO SAY IT'S ONLY A GAME,

WE SAY IT'S MORE.

TO THOSE WHO SAY IT ISN'T IF YOU WIN OR LOSE,

WE SAY IT MATTERS.

WE ARE WINNERS.

EVERY DAY.

EVERY YEAR.

PUSHING TO BE THE BEST.

WELCOME TO HILLCREST, OHIO.

Chapter
5

WE DRIVE BY the stadium, or try to. The traffic is crazy. It's like this town has a major league team.

An amplified voice blares out: *"Ladies and gentlemen, we have three hours till game time."*

People on the street cheer.

"The game, Walt. We can't be late!"

"We won't be late."

In front of the stadium are huge posters of the players. Music blasts.

You've gotta know
You've gotta know
You've gotta know
What it takes
To win.

Two kids wearing Hornets hats are dancing.

You've gotta know
You've gotta know
You've gotta know
What it takes
To win.

It takes full commitment to have this kind of attitude. The best coaches talk about dedication. I put my hand over my heart. It's totally inspiring here.

The new heart I got was from a fourteen-year-old girl who died in a bike accident in California. I had to wait for eleven months and seventeen days to get a close match. I wanted to know her name so I could write to her parents and tell them I was taking good care of their daughter's heart. Dr. Feinberg said no.

Well, I'd named my stuffed eagle Baby and my cardiac defibrillator Fred. So I named my new heart.

I call it Alice.

Do you know what *Alice* means? You're going to love this.

Noble. Possessing excellent qualities. Grand or

impressive. Having a superior mind or character.

I pat my chest. *Alice, get ready. This is going to be an awesome sixty days!*

◆　◆　◆

Walt drives past Chip Gunther's Sports Store on the corner of Hyland Road and Oakley Avenue. This store has a huge GO HORNETS banner in the window and a giant stinger jutting out from above the door.

A guy on a red motorcycle races in and out of traffic.

"Slow down, pal," Walt says to him under his breath.

The motorcycle swerves too fast around a corner.

Finally, we're on our street, Weldon Road. Walt pulls into the driveway of a small gray wooden house set back from the road and surrounded by trees.

Swoop. The Eagle has landed.

I pull down the visor in the car; I look in the mirror at my piercing brown eyes that are on fire with vision, intense determination, and the extreme love of baseball.

Lopper, I've been watching you. You've got the moves, you've got the heart, you've got the courage. I want you to go out there with the best you've got and do it . . . for your team, for your family, and for your fans, who are counting on you. It's all in there, kid. All the hours of practice, all the losses, all the wins. They've brought you to this place. Get out there and make it happen!

"The key's supposed to be under the mat, Jer."

I look in the backseat. "We're here, Jerwal."

He lights up in the box.

I get out of the car. I can hear the music from the stadium. I do the robot dance up the path, driving my shoulder down toward the ground. I move to the left and stop, to the right and stop. Jerwal and I do this together sometimes. I can see a woman looking at me from the window of the house next door. I jerk my head and freeze. She leaves the window.

It takes time to get used to me.

Walt is lugging our suitcases to the porch. "Under the mat, Jer."

I look under the mat. No key. I try the door handle. Locked.

Shoulders up, shoulders down.

We walk into the little backyard. No mat at the back door. This door is locked, too. The deck has broken steps and a sign: DO NOT USE.

Walt calls the Realtor, leaves a message, but let me tell you, this is a great yard. There's a little stream running through the back, and a wooden bridge crosses over to rocks so big you can sit on them. I walk across the bridge, plop down on a flat rock.

This will be an excellent place to sit and think.

I need to sit a lot.

But I always work to keep my head in the game.

Lopper approaches the batter's box. The crowd is on their feet. He's got one goal: to hit the ball hard and far. He fixes his mind on that, stays loose. The pitch comes . . .

"Jer!"

I get up. "Yeah?"

"I can't reach this woman!"

Walt is referring to the Realtor, but Walt also has a lot of trouble getting a date. He gets so nervous asking women out.

I walk to the front. Across the street, a girl around my age and a boy a little older are having a fight. There's a car with bumper stickers parked in their driveway.

Peace, Love, Baseball.
You are following one great coach.
Thou Shalt Respect the Game.

The license plate reads:

EL GRANDE

I like these people. I head to their yard.

The girl has long brown hair that curls below her shoulders. She is not happy.

"Bo, I swear, Mom said you need to clean the garage or she's going to set fire to all your stuff!"

Bo, the guy, throws a baseball in the air and catches it behind his back. Nice catch.

"Bo," she shouts, "do it!"

He throws the baseball up and away from him and runs to catch it. "Come on, Franny."

Her eyes turn from mad to sad. "Do you know what day this is?"

"Opening day."

"Think about it. Four years ago. What happened?"

Suddenly, Bo's eyes get sad, too. "Tell Mom I'll be right there."

Franny shouts, "It's got to be on fire for you to get it!" She heads into the house.

Bo looks at the screen door slamming shut. "I forgot, okay?" He heads to their garage.

This might not be the best time to ring the door-
bell, but being desperate . . .

I do ring it.

No answer.

I ring again.

A man shouts, "Get it, Franny!"

She opens the door. It's good I'm not like Walt, who
drops his phone around pretty females.

She waits.

I cough.

How to introduce this?

"What?" she says.

I push my hair out of my face. "Do you have a paper
clip?"

She looks at me like I'm crazy. She's got greenish eyes.

"My dad and I just moved across the street, and the
Realtor forgot to leave the key." I stick out my hand;
she looks at it. "I'm Jeremiah Lopper. We moved here
from St. Louis. I need to break into my house."

◆　◆　◆

I straighten out the paper clip. "I saw someone do this
on TV. You have to jiggle the point like this." I jiggle it

as Franny looks on. "And then, the door is supposed to open." I try that. It unlocks.

Franny looks impressed.

"It's good this works," I tell her, "but am I the only one who's nervous about how easy it is?"

She laughs. "I have to go."

"It was nice to meet you, Franny. Do you go to the middle school?"

"Yes."

"I start sixth grade on Monday."

She studies me. "Sixth grade started in September."

"Timing's not my greatest strength. How old are you?"

"Twelve," she whispers.

"I'm probably twelve, too."

She smiles strangely.

Of course, I could be older. Medical science isn't always exact.

"So this middle school—how good is it? I need the truth."

She glances at her house. "It's pretty good. The teachers are okay."

"Only okay?"

"The food in the cafeteria won't kill you."

"Is there a baseball team?"

"Kind of . . ."

"What's a 'kind of' baseball team?"

"Well . . . um . . ." She seems nervous. "Do you play?"

I hate this question. "Not exactly."

"Franny!" An older man stands on the porch and calls her.

She looks relieved. "Coming." She runs across the street. She's fast.

That could have gone worse.

It could also have gone better.

"See you Monday," I say to her back.

Where is Walt?

A dog sits on the lawn next to Franny's house and looks at me. I whistle low. The dog cocks his head, trying to decide what to do. I cock my head just like the dog, whistle again. The dog stands and almost takes a step forward.

The old woman next door pokes her head through the bushes. "That dog hasn't moved since his owner died last year."

The dog has black and white markings like a spaniel.

You can do this, dog.

"Who are you?" the woman asks.

"I'm Jeremiah Lopper, ma'am. My dad and I just moved here from St. Louis."

She pinches up her face. "Penelope Prim."

"Nice to meet you."

I look at the dog. "You can come if you want."

The dog leans forward, but doesn't come.

Walt walks around from the backyard. "I still can't get the Realtor."

I point to the open door.

"How do you do these things, Jer?"

I show him the straightened paper clip.

He carries his suitcase inside. "I'm grateful you use your gifts for good."

Chapter

6

HARGIE CANTWELL HAS a sting in his slider. It whizzes and dunks past the batter for the Temple High School Tigers, who stands there, clueless.

"Strike three!" the umpire calls.

The crowd in the Hornets' stadium goes crazy and makes a loud buzzing sound. People wearing Hornets hats shake their heads to make the stingers bounce.

Hargie's struck out the last two batters with only seven pitches. That's impressive. It's the sixth inning.

"He's a big kid," Walt says, "but he's going to blow out his arm at those speeds."

Walt pitched in college, but his arm didn't hold up.

Wham! Another strike.

Buzzzzzzzzzzzzzzzzzzzzzzzzzzzzzzzzzzzzzzzzzzzzz.

We stand up, we sit down.

Let's go, Hornets!
clap clap
clap clap clap

Turns out Hargie Cantwell can hit, too. He sits on a three-one fastball and whacks it into the stands for a two-run homer.

"That kid is something," Walt says.

I grin at Walt. It is so amazing to be here.

Behind us, two men talk about the Hornets catcher being suspended because he insulted the Spanish teacher. I don't know if the insult was in Spanish or English, but the principal sent him home for a week, and that meant he couldn't play on opening day.

One man says, "You know what that principal told Coach Perkins?"

"What?"

"That woman said baseball wasn't as important as respectful behavior. Can you imagine that?"

"They'll remember it when her contract's up for renewal."

Walt and I look at each other.

I see Franny in the crowd, cheering, twirling a GO HORNETS towel.

I wish I could play. I used to play when I was little. Third base. Shortstop.

I'm still hoping medical science is going to figure me out.

Aunt Charity wanted me to write a three-paragraph essay about that. I didn't need three paragraphs to talk about it. I only had one thing to say:

I deal with it.
The End

In the margin, she wrote: *Jeremiah, you do indeed deal with it. I give you an A+ for courage and an Incomplete on content, which, believe me, is generous.*

I rewrote it in three paragraphs, but I basically said the same thing.

◆ ◆ ◆

The Hornets have a huge lead: 11–2. In the final inning Hargie throws his glove down and starts screaming when a kid from the Tigers drives in a run. Hargie is stomping and fuming on the mound like he's lost the game. The catcher runs up and tries to calm him down; the coach runs up, puts his arm around Hargie, and talks to him for a while. He throws some out-of-control pitches, but then he settles down and finishes the inning. The Hornets win 11–3.

After the game, I try to find Franny, but she's disappeared into the crowd. Walt and I stand in line and finally get into Junk Ball Pizza—this is only okay pizza, but it seems to be the place to go after the game. A few of the Hornets come in and people applaud them like superstars. There's a special booth with a sign: ALWAYS RESERVED FOR COACH PERKINS. No one is sitting there.

We head home. We pull up our driveway and walk inside the house to the kitchen. Walt leans against the refrigerator. He does this when his back hurts. He straightens himself against the door.

A loud motorcycle goes down the street; we hear what sounds like our neighbor Mrs. Prim shout, "Hargie Cantwell, if you don't slow down on that blasted thing, you'll kill yourself or somebody else!"

"I guess it's hard to come down from a big game like that, Walt."

Walt rubs his lower back. "That guy is wound too tight."

Chapter 7

I'D JUST SAY to every kid who doesn't want to go to school, if you'd been sick for a few years and couldn't go much, like me, you might think about the whole experience differently.

I'm standing by the NO BULLYING/NO KIDDING poster in the office of Hillcrest Middle School. The lady at the desk looks at my too-long doctor's report, then at me. I try to look healthy.

I wish people didn't have to know about my heart. Mention the word *transplant* and people get nervous. It's not like I had a brain transplant!

"How do we know if something goes wrong?" is her question.

I'd like to say, "My chest rings."

Walt puts his hand on my shoulder. "It shouldn't be

a problem, but you have my emergency line. That will get me anywhere." Walt's emergency line blares like a siren. "And the doctor has requested that he carry his phone in school for emergencies. He won't abuse the privilege."

She stares at me. I hold up my right hand like I'm being sworn in. "I won't. I swear. Unless I'm dying, no one will ever see the phone." Still staring. "But I have no immediate plans for death." Walt shakes his head.

I'm looking at a door with a yellow-and-black sign. There's a big exclamation mark in a triangle— underneath it is one word: HAZARD. A man walks out of that office. The woman says, "Mr. Hazard, this is Jeremiah, our new student."

We shake hands.

"Mr. Hazard," she continues, "is our vice principal."

The lady hands him my medical report. He leafs through the pages, then looks at me.

"It's not as bad as it seems, sir."

Mr. Hazard smiles. A woman walks up who looks official. "Dr. Selligman," Mr. Hazard says, "meet Jeremiah, our new student."

"Hello, Jeremiah."

"Dr. Selligman is the principal," Mr. Hazard adds.

I stand straighter. First impressions are important. "This seems like a good school," I say.

Dr. Selligman smiles. "I'm glad to hear that. I hope you'll jump right in."

"Yes, ma'am. I'd like to do that."

"Any questions so far?"

"Is there a middle school baseball team?"

The principal looks at Mr. Hazard like she's not sure. Mr. Hazard coughs. "Ah, somewhat. We don't exactly have a full team." He pauses. "That program . . . is being reevaluated."

"Well, I have a meeting. Glad you're here, Jeremiah." Dr. Selligman heads to her office.

Mr. Hazard gives my medical report back to the lady at the desk. "And my door is always open. Welcome to our school."

He marches out of the office. Actually, I have another question.

What's a "somewhat" baseball team?

The lady says she'll take me to my first period English class. Walt is working hard to not look worried.

I whisper to him, "I'll try to blend in."

He laughs and pats me on the back.

◆ ◆ ◆

I sit in the middle row of sixth grade English class and hear the dreaded words.

"The three-paragraph essay," Mrs. Ogletree says, "has a simple structure."

Aunt Charity drummed this into me and it will never leave. When I'm old and bald and can't remember my name, I will remember the three-part structure.

Introduction
Body
Conclusion

Mrs. Ogletree writes on the board:

Introduction
Body
Conclusion

I can tell she's lost some of the kids already.

"Let's talk about what's in each of those parts," she says. "In an introduction, you present the concept or the thesis you want to get across."

Slumped shoulders in the class—at least the kids in front of me are slumping.

"What's a thesis?"

I know this.

No one is raising their hands.

Mrs. Ogletree stares at the class until a boy can't stand the silence anymore. He raises his hand. She points at him. "Donald."

"Uh, a thesis . . . is kind of like an idea." He has a flat voice.

"That's right . . ." She wants more, though, and this teacher can wait. Kids are looking down. I don't want to raise my hand on the first day, but I don't have any choice. She nods at me.

"A thesis is like a theory," I say. "It's an idea you have, and you need to explain it and build on it."

Everyone looks at me.

"Very good, Gerard."

"It's Jeremiah, ma'am."

I can't believe that the three-paragraph essay has followed me to Ohio!

Or the recorder.

In Music Appreciation, twenty kids with recorders

are trying to play "Go Tell Aunt Rhody," which makes me want to run out of the room, it's so grim. I've got this song down like some kids know "Chopsticks" on the piano.

"You're quite good at the recorder, Jerry," Mrs. Nimroy says.

I mention it's Jeremiah, not Jerry. I don't mention that only Walt is allowed to call me Jer.

It's good to know the stuff you learn has applications in other places.

It's less good when it's not the stuff you care about.

◆ ◆ ◆

I've been looking for Franny all day. I see her in the cafeteria sitting at a table with other girls. She has a tray of red velvet cupcakes with white frosting.

I walk up. "I'm Jeremiah, the interesting new kid. Remember? You brought these cupcakes for my first day?"

She laughs. "It's my birthday. Today I'm twelve."

I meet her friend Lilah, who is in charge of the cupcakes. If I stare at them long enough, I bet I'll get one.

"Would you like a cupcake . . . Jeremiah?"

I sit down. "I would." I turn to Franny. "You need to do something fantastic. No, beyond amazing, for your birthday. You can never take a birthday for granted." I'm big on birthdays, since mine is a theory.

"My grandpa is taking me to a Cincinnati Reds game tonight."

That's a celebration, and this is an excellent cupcake. "Where are you sitting?"

"The bleachers. We always sit there."

"That's good, Franny. You learn a lot about life in the bleachers."

One of the girls at the table asks me, "Where are you from?"

"Well, it's a secret planet that hasn't been discovered yet."

All the girls laugh. I finish the top on my cupcake, then attack the bottom.

"It's called St. Louis," Franny mentions.

"That's just a cover," I assure her.

❖ ❖ ❖

Franny and I take the bus home from school together. It pulls onto our street. The dog I whistled at yesterday is watching.

"You've got a name, I bet," I shout to the dog.

"It's Adler," Franny tells me.

"Adler, come."

Adler sits there studying me. I whistle like yesterday. I have to whistle three times, but the third time works. Adler pads over.

"That is totally amazing, Jeremiah!"

"So what's your story, Adler?" I get down on one knee and rub this dog's neck, then move under his chin. "My dog, Digger, loved this." The dog wags its tail. It looks part spaniel, part something else. "Are you a combo plate?"

Franny laughs. The dog sits there.

I don't know what I am, either. It's okay. You can still have a good life.

An older man walks out of Franny's house, followed by a lady who looks like Franny. The man says, "Son, how did you get that dog over there?"

"I whistled."

The man and the lady walk over. He's got a wide forehead, a wide nose, and smiling eyes. "That must've been some whistle. That dog hasn't budged since his owner died. He keeps waiting for old Bob Simon to come home from work; he only goes into the house at night. We all take turns feeding him."

He gives the dog a pat. Adler looks back across the street at his yard.

"Yeah, you made the journey finally, didn't you, boy?" The man sticks out his hand. I shake it firmly. "Ellis Grand. Franny's grandfather."

"Also known as El Grande," Franny says.

"That's a great name, sir."

"I coached baseball a while back and the players called me that."

"Wow. That's, like, the ultimate. I'm Jeremiah Lopper."

"Welcome to Hillcrest, son. Are you a baseball man?"

"I'm a maniac, sir."

The lady says, "You two will get along just fine. I'm Val Engers, Franny's mom."

I shake her hand, too. "Have fun at the game tonight."

Franny's grandpa smiles. "Should be a good one."

"I think the Reds will win, sir. The Cubs weren't hitting strong against left-handed pitchers in spring training, and Cincinnati's starter has wicked breaking stuff. Plus with their midwinter trades and the two kids up from Triple-A, the manager's finally got the lineup right."

Franny's mom laughs. "Are we ready for you, Jeremiah?"

Possibly not.

"You play ball, son?"

I hate this question. "Not right now."

He points at me. "We'll talk again."

They climb into their car and head off.

There goes . . .

EL GRANDE

Happy birthday, Franny.

Adler cocks his head and looks at me. I rub him behind the ears. "Adler, I really like it here."

Chapter
8

"JERWAL, HOW WAS your day?"

Jerwal glows and beeps.

"Yeah, mine too."

I'm in our kitchen getting dinner ready. I have a few no-fail menus. Tonight I'm making chicken sausages with sautéed apples and salad, and multitasking this with homework.

The three-paragraph essay. Ideas to write about:

- Living with Robots (Jerwal's favorite)
- What Eagles Can Teach Us (Baby's favorite)
- The Intense Power of Baseball to Transform Life as We Know It (my favorite)
- Being a New Kid at School (probably the teacher's favorite)

I get the sausages out, slice the apples. I take a minute to put up my robot poster that I made for the fourth grade science fair. I couldn't go to the fair, I was too sick, but Jerwal went and he was a big hit. On the poster, I summed up Isaac Asimov's first law of robotics: "A robot must protect humans and may not injure them."

I showed pictures of good robots through the ages, including Jerwal. I had photos of how Walt and I built him. I won third prize and got the school's Inspiration Award.

Jerwal is the ultimate robot who protects and doesn't injure. He was there for me when I was in the hospital. I told him everything, even things I wouldn't tell Walt. I told him every time I was afraid, every time I got side effects from the medicine they gave me. He'd glow in the dark, which was comforting. A robot is an excellent listener.

The nurses got used to this. One nurse told him about her cheating ex-boyfriend, and Jerwal glowed at just the right times and beeped sensitively.

I put out all my medicine on the counter—I have eight kinds of pills and I need to take them on time.

My phone dings three times a day to remind me, then Jerwal makes a backup noise so I won't forget.

My phone buzzes. It's Aunt Charity calling.

Her worried face fills the screen.

I gulp meds. "Hi," I say. I click so she can see me.

"You look pale," she announces.

"I'm fine. Really."

"Are you napping?"

"I was about to take one." This is absolutely true. I was going to take a twelve-minute nap like John F. Kennedy did. He was a famous power napper even in the White House.

I tell her about school.

"Are you using your antiseptic?"

I nod.

"How is your blood pressure?"

"I take the medicine." High blood pressure is a side effect of the medicine I'm taking.

"And where is your father?"

I walk the phone over to the stove and show her the great dinner I made.

"Sausage," she announces, "has additives and—"

"It's organic." I have to eat healthy—doctor's orders.

Walt, thankfully, comes in the door. "And have you had a bowel movement, young man?"

"Not since last month."

She gasps.

"He's kidding!" Walt grabs the phone and glares at me. "Seriously, we are doing well."

I'm glad to have an aunt, even though she can drive me this side of crazy.

"I think we should talk daily," she says.

I shake my head, which is Jerwal's sign to shake his head, too. I do a little robot dance. Jerwal jerks his arms up and down.

"Maybe we should talk weekly, Char. How are you?"

She doesn't want to talk about that. But then she says, "Tell Jeremiah they're lucky to have him at that school."

She means it, too. I shout, "Thanks, Aunt Charity."

Call over.

Walt and I eat in the kitchen with the Reds game on the radio.

Don't mess up, you guys—it's Franny's big day.

Walt's loving the dinner.

"How are the robots at work, Walt?"

"You can see for yourself." He opens his backpack, takes out an orange ball with a flat side, and puts it on the floor.

"That's a robot?"

"Yep. This is SARB. Search and Report Back. We're developing them for police and fire departments." Computer out, he types something. "Find trouble, SARB."

The orange ball moves, stops at the screen door, and falls over on its back like a turtle. This happens two times.

"Why does it do that, Walt?"

"It's not clear." He's typing more.

"Can Jerwal meet it?"

"Not yet."

"It might need a friend, Walt."

"There are dozens just like it at the office."

Uncle Jack didn't like robots because he said they can't take a joke. Walt and I tried to program Jerwal to make a ha-ha noise, but it sounded more like he was wheezing.

Walt opens the screen door. "Find trouble, SARB."

The little robot rolls onto the porch. We follow it. There's a noise in the bushes. Mrs. Prim is staring at us.

I see no point in lying. "Mrs. Prim, this is my father, Walt. And this is his robot, SARB."

Her face twists up.

Walt tips his baseball cap to her. "It's a lovely evening, ma'am. Nice to meet you."

He picks SARB up. Moths dance by the porch light. The Reds just made a very stupid error, letting a Cub get to second, but they're still ahead by two runs.

Walt does the dishes. I arrange my baseball and coaching books on the bookshelf in my room. It sags a little under the weight. Jerwal is in the corner getting a power zap. That's what I need—a power cord to plug into.

Today in study hall, I researched Coach Perkins, the Hornets coach. He has a lot of big coach sayings:

"I don't believe in losing. I believe in winning. One hundred percent."

"I eat winning for breakfast. I drink it, I breathe it. Every minute. Every day. I program myself to go for it."

"This is what I tell my players: you play for me, you leave your doubts at the door."

The door opens and SARB comes rolling in.

"Walt!"

"Act natural, Jer. He needs practice getting around things."

SARB goes up to my suitcase and stops.

"It's got my stuff," I tell it.

SARB seems stuck. "Do you want me to turn you around?" I reach down and pick the little robot up.

"I'm getting an emergency signal, Jer! He has to do it himself."

I put SARB down. "Sorry!"

I'd make eye contact if SARB had reasonable eyes. "You're a winner, SARB. Every minute. Every day. Walt will program you to leave your doubts at the door."

SARB backs up, runs smack into the door, and falls over.

◆ ◆ ◆

The sign Walt put up on the door reads:

NO ROBOTS IN THE BATHROOM
by order of The Management

I look at Jerwal and SARB. "I'm sorry, you guys. Walt has this boundary thing."

I open the bathroom door and walk in. It's pink, unfortunately.

There's a small mirror above the sink. I look at myself. People say I look like a kid actor, with my straight blond hair that falls over my left eye. I brush the hair back. My eyes look tough today. My skin isn't puffy like it used to be when I was sick. It definitely isn't blue—it got a little blue when my heart was at its worst.

Lopper, you're looking good, kid. You're looking strong. Go warm up. I'm putting you in the game.

I take out my phone, type:

```
NOTE TO SELF: FIND OUT—Does this
school have a baseball team? "Kind
of," "somewhat," is not an answer.
```

Chapter
9

"DOES THIS SCHOOL have a baseball team?"

I ask three kids on the bus and get three answers.

Yes.

No.

Maybe.

"Does this school have a football team?"

Well, yeah.

"A basketball team?"

Of course.

"Track, soccer . . . ?"

Sure.

"So what's with baseball?"

Kids shrug, except for a guy named Logo Larson. The school bus drives past the Hornets' Nest. Logo points out the window. "If you don't win here, nothing else matters."

"You mean the middle school team didn't win?" I ask.

"We won." He rubs his elbow and stares out the window.

I say, "I don't understand."

He shrugs and keeps looking out the window.

◆　◆　◆

The bus pulls around the middle school baseball diamond. The field doesn't look like it's been used much. The grass is overgrown; the pitcher's mound is a mess. I see Franny and a few girls running laps. Franny is in the lead, running fast and easy. The bus pulls up to the middle school entrance. Mr. Hazard is in front saying good morning.

He gives me a wave. "How's it going, Jeremiah?"

I smile and walk over. "Good, sir. I have another question."

"Shoot."

"What's a 'somewhat' baseball team?"

His smile cracks a little. "You know, that's a good question, but unfortunately, it would take too long to bring you up to speed. You're not thinking of playing, right?"

"Right."

"Next year, hopefully."

"I won't be here next year."

"Of course." He pats me on the back.

◆ ◆ ◆

"Does this school have a baseball team?" I ask Ms. Mullner, the science teacher.

"Well, I don't think they do, Jeremiah. This is my first year teaching. They used to have one and something happened."

Logo, the kid from the bus, says, "The coach got fired," and takes his seat.

I sit next to him. "Why did they fire him?"

"He pushed too hard."

I whisper. "What do you mean?"

"Nobody wanted to play for him anymore."

Ms. Mullner is standing by her desk. "Today," she says, "we're going to be talking about huge small things: molecules. How can we explain something so infinitesimal?"

No kids raise their hands.

"Anybody hungry?"

A few hands go up.

Ms. Mullner holds a sandwich. "Salami, cheese,

turkey, ham, on a roll. What happens when I cut it?" She cuts it once, then again and again until the parts are so small, they fall apart.

I raise my hand. "You can't call it a sandwich anymore."

"That's right." She cuts it some more and holds up a crumb of bread. "A molecule is the smallest particle of a substance that still retains the properties of the substance. And the things molecules are made up of are called atoms."

A tall, skinny boy says, "You ruined the sandwich."

"All in the name of science," she explains.

This is so much better than the three-paragraph essay, but not nearly as important as baseball.

◆ ◆ ◆

I am sitting on the bleachers by the middle school baseball diamond watching four guys play catch. They're actually pretty good. Two of them were in my science class.

The tall, skinny guy has a good arm, throwing fast to the shortest guy, who jumps up to catch it and doesn't miss. He turns around fast and throws it to an African American kid, who scoops it up and shouts, "Wake up, Lopez!" and throws it long to the fourth guy, who says, "I'm awake, Terrell!" and blasts it back.

The good news: these guys have accuracy and hustle—two big pluses in serious baseball.

The not-so-good news: there are only four of them. You need nine players for a team, plus a few extra.

A toss high and away. The first guy runs, catches the ball, and tosses it fast to the second guy.

I'm waiting for the rest of the somewhat/kind of team. Franny shows up holding the hand of a younger boy with curly dark hair who looks at the sky and smiles, then looks at the guys playing catch and smiles. This kid is just happy to be here.

"Hey, Benny Man," the tall guy says. "Whaddya know?"

Benny holds up his glove.

"Excellent, man." The tall guy throws a sizzler to the short kid, who leaps to catch it.

"Great catch!" Benny shouts, and he throws his glove in the air, tries to catch it, but doesn't come close. Benny is on his knees now looking at something on the ground.

Franny says, "You want your snack, Benny?"

"I want my snack, Benny." He giggles and walks over.

She takes out a lunch box and opens it. "Your mom

was out of oranges today, so she gave you apples. Okay?"

Benny's face changes. He shakes his head no.

"They're good apples. My favorite."

Benny throws down his glove. "Only oranges. Only oranges."

"I understand, Benny. We'll get them later."

He shakes his head again really hard. He looks like he might start crying.

I stand up and say, "I've got an orange." I walk over, take the orange out of my book bag, and give it to the kid.

Franny smiles. "Benny, this is Jeremiah, our new neighbor."

I stick out my hand to shake Benny's; he puts both his hands behind him.

"Benny, that's not polite. Jeremiah is our new friend. He lives on our street and he gave you his orange. He gave you a present."

Benny is hunched over now, trying to get the skin off the orange.

"I'll show you a secret of how to do that." I hold out my hand. "I need the orange just for a second. I'll give it back."

Benny looks at my hand, at the orange, at Franny,

who nods. He drops the orange in my hand.

"Watch this," I tell him. I see two other guys come to play ball. One guy is doing a practice swing with a bat; the other is crouching down like a catcher.

I rub the orange round and round in my hands to loosen the skin. Walt taught me this. Then I peel it and it comes right off.

Benny claps.

I break the orange into sections and hand them to him. He holds them like I just gave him money.

"Wow," he says.

Franny pushes a paper plate toward him. "Put them here, Benny."

Benny makes a flower pattern with them on the plate.

"That's pretty," Franny says.

"Pretty," Benny says. "I'm forty-two."

I laugh. "You don't look that old, Benny."

He doesn't connect with that.

"Benny is eight." Franny hands him an orange section.

So, what's your story, Benny?

I hear, "You gonna pitch, Sky, or are you gonna stand there?"

I turn to look at the field. The tall, skinny guy, Sky,

says, "I'm gonna pitch. Don't blink, you'll miss it."

He does a windmill warm-up. The batter bounces a little, waiting for the throw. Logo, the kid I met on the bus, is catcher. He makes a signal. Sky nods a little and lets one loose, missing the plate by, I'd say, a mile.

"Settle down," Logo tells him.

The batter waits. Sky brings his right arm up and snaps the ball in the dirt.

Benny arranges his sandwich around the orange pieces and puts his carrots in a line on his napkin. He opens his little box of raisins and puts five raisins inside the orange.

"Come on, Sky!" the catcher shouts.

Sky lifts his right arm, pushes off on his foot, and gets the ball closer to the plate, but not close enough.

I look at Franny, who is handing Benny a box of juice with a straw. "This is the baseball team?"

"This is the baseball team," she says.

"Great catch!" Benny shouts.

"Way to go, Benny Man!" Sky shouts back.

"They need nine guys to play," I mention.

She bends Benny's straw. "They need nine people, Jeremiah. They don't all have to be guys."

True. I walk on the field. We need to get this moving. "You're good," I tell them.

They like that.

"I think, Sky, you've got power; you need to keep your eyes focused on the catcher's glove and change your release point. Release the ball a little earlier. You're hanging on to it too long."

Sky doesn't like that. "Who are you?"

"Jeremiah Lopper. Try it, Sky."

He stands there, looks around.

"Come on." Logo crouches down, holds his glove. "Right in here, guy."

"Let the ball go earlier," I remind him.

Sky does a warm-up, lets the ball go, and *wham*.

I nod. "That's a strike."

The guys look impressed.

"You play?" the black kid asks me.

"I used to. I coach now."

They laugh.

They can laugh.

"We're looking for a coach who's a little taller." Logo breaks up at that.

"Shut up, Logo," Terrell warns. "What do you mean, you coach?"

"I mean, if people are interested, I can really help you play better."

Even though I just improved their game, I can see they need time to process this.

I look toward the little hill and the big, shiny baseball bat statue. I grab my book bag. "Gotta go."

Chapter

10

"YOU LOOK TIRED," Walt mentions. "Did you overdo yesterday?"

"I'm napping."

Walt pulls the car onto the freeway. "Your eyes are open and you're talking."

"Eagles never shut their eyes."

"They don't speak, either."

It's eleven a.m. I had to leave school early for an appointment. We are headed to see my new cardiologist, Dr. Dugan, who won't be my cardiologist for very long, but I'm hoping she'll give it everything she's got.

"I can't sleep." I tell him about the baseball mystery at school. "I don't know what's going on, Walt."

He merges into the middle lane. "I do."

"You do?"

"One of the guys I work with told me. His son was on the team."

"What did he say?"

Walt turns off the radio. "He said they'd had a serious ball club. It was a feeder team for the Hornets. The kids worked hard, and the coach, a guy named Bordin, pushed them hard. Travel baseball. Camp. Year-round stuff to keep in shape. Total focus. Some kids handled it, but then the coach pushed beyond it—kids were burning out, getting injured, playing hurt. Parents were not happy. The winning got to be too much. A lot of kids dropped out. Bordin got fired and didn't leave quietly."

"What did he do, Walt?"

"I don't know. A few of the kids still meet after school to play, but they don't have enough for a team. There's a group of parents who got turned off to baseball."

"That's terrible."

"I agree."

"Do you think the school wants to do something?"

Walt parks the car. "I have a feeling some of the parents would fight that."

"It's not baseball's fault, Walt!"

I take out my phone and look up "Coach Bordin Hillcrest." There's an angry picture of him, and below that, there's this: *I was doing the job I was hired to do!*

Walt pulls into the hospital lot and parks the car. "Ready?"

We get out of the car, walk to the entrance. We head to the elevator, and it's like I'm back at the hospital in St. Louis. Memories come rushing at me.

We waited almost a year for me to get a new heart—a donor heart, they call it. Every day my bag was packed, every day we checked the phone again and again. You give up; you believe; you try not to think about it— sometimes it's all you can think about. And when they called and said, "We have a heart for you," we had to go right away. I felt so lucky. Not everyone who needs a new heart gets one. There aren't enough to go around.

"You're going to make it through, Jer." That's what Walt told me right before the surgery. "Be brave now. I'll see you soon."

The nurse came in. "Jeremiah, they're ready for you in OR."

I wasn't sure I was ready for them, but I'd studied being brave. The people who are good at it, like Walt, seemed to focus on a good outcome, not on the stuff that can go wrong.

I pictured myself with my new heart, running to catch a pop fly; hitting a liner into the gap; sliding into second base; and squeezing out a double. But when I got into the operating room, all that courage went splat. I started to cry. I said, "I need my dad."

Some brave kid.

Dr. Feinberg said, "Jeremiah. Look at me." I tried to do that and not look at what was happening around him. "We know exactly what to do."

That calmed me down. They put me to sleep. That's all I remember, and when I woke up, all I could think was, *I made it.*

I had a ventilator to help me breathe and tubes in my chest. But that didn't matter.

I made it!

◆ ◆ ◆

"The doctor will see you now."

Dr. Sarah Dugan has the same plastic heart on her desk that Dr. Feinberg has on his desk. Walt drops his phone when we come in.

I smile at the heart—it feels like home. "Is there a catalog for these things?" I ask her.

"Yes." She pushes back her blonde hair. "Cardiologist shirts, cards, ties, socks, posters." She holds up a coffee mug: JUST LIKE THE OTHER DOCTORS, ONLY SMARTER.

Okay, I like you.

Walt laughs and drops his phone again.

Did I mention she's also pretty?

She's looking through my file. "How are you feeling?"

"Okay."

"Since we've just met, Jeremiah, you need to define 'okay.'"

"I didn't sleep all that well last night. I'm a little tired, but I'm dealing with it."

"Any chest pain?"

"No."

She walks over to where I'm sitting on the examining table. She puts her hand over my heart, presses.

"Any pain?"

"No."

She keeps her hand there, puts her other hand on my back. "Cough, please."

I do.

"Any pain?"

"No."

She listens to my heart with her stethoscope, then goes through my chart. "Tell me about the transplant."

Even though it's right in front of their faces on the report, doctors want you to repeat everything. I mention the virus. The cardiomyopathy. "I almost died. And then the new heart had problems."

"There was some rejection initially," Walt tells her, "and we were told that weakened the transplant."

"When was that?"

"A week after my tenth birthday."

She looks up from the chart. "When's your birthday?"

I look at Walt. *Do we need to go into all that?*

Walt gives her the fast version.

I add, "It's why we don't look alike, right down to our noses."

She puts my report down and smiles. "A nose doesn't make you part of a family, Jeremiah. It's the heart."

I like that.

"Thank you," Walt says to her.

She asks me, "What are your goals, Jeremiah?"

Great question!

I mention running and having energy and not being limited by anything in the universe.

"And I want to coach, you know? I want to coach baseball, because it's one of the big things I focused on when I was sick. I loved it before—Walt and I have that in common. But even when I couldn't play, I'd run the game in my head. Every day I'd think about holding the bat and all the things it takes to be a winner."

I know she's studying me without saying it.

"I wasn't going to give up—I wasn't going to let myself even think about doing that."

She nods. "Do you get down at all, Jeremiah?"

I move a little. Walt looks at me. Dr. Dugan checks my reflexes.

"How about that feeling down question?" she asks.

"Maybe a little."

"What happens when you run?"

"I just get dizzy and I have to stop. My heart beats too fast."

"Do you feel down when you run?"

"I haven't tried running for a while. I don't know."

"When you first had the transplant, after the initial healing phase, could you run?"

"Not really. I didn't believe it, though. I wanted it so bad."

"What happened?" Her hair is short and she has freckles on her nose. I've never had a doctor with freckles—Dr. Feinberg has a mole on his nose. "Did you try to run?"

"Yes." They look at me; I feel I have to defend myself. "I was playing baseball. These kids asked if I could play in the outfield. They said no one in the league was good enough to hit out there, so I was standing—I swear! Just trying to keep my head in the game, and this big kid cracks one and it's coming to me, but actually it's over my head, and I start running to catch it. I missed it. It rolled all the way back to this tree and I ran to get it, then I threw it to third base. And my heart felt like it was going to beat out of my chest. I got sick."

I'm beginning to feel that way now.

"I shouldn't have played, I know! I just wanted to be out there. I wanted to run!"

Dr. Dugan is studying my face. "We're going to get some blood tests. Okay?"

"Okay."

"And I want you to wear a heart monitor for a few weeks."

"I've done that before."

"So you know it makes you smarter."

"Absolutely!" I also know I take it off when I shower.

"Then we'll have a good map to follow." She writes something on the report. "I appreciate how much you love baseball and how you wanted to run."

"I still want to run."

"I hear that. How are you feeling now?" she asks.

I stand up. "Good."

"Touch your toes."

I do that.

"Jump up and down three times."

I do that.

"Dizzy?"

"No."

Dr. Dugan looks at my chart. "Twirl around and speak German."

I laugh.

Walt laughs really long.

"You're doing quite well." She shakes my hand. "I'll review this with the transplant team. They'll be here at your next visit. A pleasure to meet you, Jeremiah Lopper." She shakes Walt's hand. "More to come."

◆ ◆ ◆

"I like her, Walt. She's smart and funny. You noticed?"

Walt nods.

"You dropped your phone a lot."

"Once, Jer."

Twice, actually.

"Walt. Listen. I'm sorry how complicated all this—"

"Let me tell you something. I couldn't be a good father to some run-of-the-mill, ordinary kid. I would drive them crazy. I work on complex systems, Jer."

I'm a complex system, all right! I've got electrodes on my chest. They come with the heart monitor. I'm naming it Boxter.

"Should I call the insurance company, Walt?"

We take turns at this. Walt has coached me on what to say. I dial the 800 number, wait forever, then get a woman's voice. I lower my voice to sound super mature and explain I'll have a new cardiologist for two months and want them to know. She says we owe them money from the last doctor's bill. We paid it. We always do and somehow something always goes wrong.

"Ma'am, we've had this insurance for ten years now, we never miss a monthly payment, my diagnosis has been documented, and your company keeps refusing to pay for treatment that is covered in our plan. The last letter we received from you asked if I got this condition as the result of an accident at work. I'm twelve. I don't go to work." I take a deep breath. "And the letter was in Spanish."

I cover the receiver. "She's getting her manager, Walt."

Chapter
11

WALT AND I are driving past the Hornets' Nest. They have a big game tomorrow. A life-size poster of Coach Perkins is above the entrance.

They're sure into hero worship here.

Coach Perkins has blue eyes and a half-bald head. His jaw seems like it's cut out of rock.

I wonder what he says to his team to get them motivated before a big game.

I wonder why the middle school team had so many problems.

Walt looks at me. "You okay?"

"Yeah."

I put my head against the car window like I'm resting. Resting is a difficult concept for me, because my mind is always going fifteen places at once.

I wonder what Yaff is doing . . .

I wonder if Franny and I can ever be good friends . . .

I wonder what my test results are going to show . . .

I wonder where my real mother is . . .

That's a big jump from test results, I know, but I wonder if she thinks about me.

She's got to. If she's still alive, that is . . .

She said I was her best boy. I'm working hard to prove that.

◆ ◆ ◆

It's a little cold tonight, but not too cold to eat dinner on the porch, although I do wear an extra fleece just in case. Walt and I sit here finishing our veggie pizza. There's a wind chime shaped like a bird that's dinging away. Adler is eating dog chow from a bowl we put out for him. In a little while he'll go inside his house to be with Mr. Simon's widow. Franny said Mrs. Simon can't get out much anymore. Adler finishes eating and looks at the street, waiting for Mr. Simon to come home.

I tell him, "Adler, you're beyond loyal, but you're waiting for something that's gone forever." Adler looks at me. I rub his head. "You must have loved your friend a lot, boy."

Adler sighs and lies down. I'm watching Bo, across

the street, throw his baseball up in the air and catch it. There's some junk from the garage in a pile on the street—a broken basketball hoop, an old trampoline, a large cardboard chicken that needs explanation. El Grande is reading his paper on the porch. A few minutes ago, Benny and his mother brought us a plate of homemade chocolate cookies to welcome us to the neighborhood. It's seven o'clock. Franny comes out of her house as an old car drives slowly by, honking.

The driver keeps honking like something's wrong.

Walt and I stand up.

Adler stops eating.

The car stops in the middle of the road. Old Mrs. Prim gets out, waving her hands. "Oh, Lord help us!" she cries, and heads to Franny's house screaming, "Ellis!"

El Grande is standing now, too.

"Ellis! My God . . ."

Benny's mother runs out of her house. "Penny, are you all right?"

Walt and I head across the street to help.

El Grande walks down the steps toward her. "What happened?"

"Ellis! You heard . . . ?"

"Heard what?" He leads her to his porch to sit down, but she doesn't want to do that. "Penny. Talk to me."

She looks at Benny's mother. "Claire . . ."

"What happened, dear?"

Mrs. Prim's face is caved in; her eyes are wet. She's trying to catch her breath. "It's Hargie." Tears run down her old face.

Bo runs over. "What happened?"

Mrs. Prim heads for the porch step now, shaking her head like she can't believe it. "He rode his motorcycle home from practice. He parked it in the garage like always. And he keeled over . . . right there."

Franny's mother rushes out the door.

Benny's mother says, "Oh, no!"

Mrs. Prim lowers her head, weeping. "I'm sorry to tell you all, but Hargie's . . . dead."

"What?" El Grande whispers.

Mrs. Prim nods. "The sheriff's mother told me. It's terrible."

Bo opens his mouth, but nothing comes out.

Franny grabs on to the porch rail.

Benny's mother puts her hand to her heart.

I look at Walt. It's like a truck fell from the sky.

We stand there, frozen.

Chapter
12

FLOWERS PILE UP at the Hornets' Nest stadium.

The *Hillcrest Herald* brings out a special edition.

HARGIE CANTWELL DIES
17-Year-Old Was the Winningest Pitcher
in Hornets History
A Town Mourns

I didn't know him, but when you read about someone, when you know how fast he threw and how many batters he struck out and how tall he was (six foot one) and how much he weighed (210 pounds), it feels like you know him.

He had a heart attack—that's what people are saying.

A boy that young and strong . . .

I know that hearts can fool you. People don't think

there's a thing wrong, and then it's too late.

It's like a giant vacuum came and sucked up all the energy in Hillcrest.

"He probably had some kind of undiagnosed heart condition," a man whispers behind me. "It happens to young athletes—they get dehydrated, stressed. No one sees it coming."

I touch an electrode and look at the stained glass windows filtering in the light.

Walt and I are at Peaceful Lutheran Church with the rest of the town. Cars are double-parked on the street—there's no more room in the parking lot.

Maybe if Hargie had worn a heart monitor, he'd still be alive. I've never been to a funeral like this.

The high school chorus sings, or tries to.

Hargie's father stands up front and tries to say a few words, but he lowers his head and can't go on.

I look over at Franny, who is crying; Bo is folded forward in the church pew. Their mom is sitting with her eyes closed. El Grande is looking at his hands.

Sometimes loss is a thing so thick, it hangs in the air.

I am sitting next to a woman who is sneezing, and this isn't good. I try to lean toward Walt because I have to avoid germs.

I hate even thinking about it at a time like this!

Walt and I change places on the pew. He's like that, my dad, always protecting me.

Pastor Burmeister's voice cracks as he leads us in the Twenty-Third Psalm.

Walt puts his hand on my shoulder. We prayed this before my transplant surgery. We prayed so hard.

The Lord is my shepherd;
I shall not want.
He makes me to lie down in green pastures;
He leads me beside the still waters;
He restores my soul.

We finish saying the psalm together.

There's a hush as a big teenage boy comes forward. His eyes are red from crying. He unfolds a piece of paper and stands there looking at it; then he reads.

"Hargie, you were my best friend. You knew that. I hope you knew I always wanted to be like you, to play like you. You always gave it all you had in every game, in every practice. We practiced for years, you and me. I'd always be the one who got tired first, and you always wanted to keep going. You always outlasted me . . ." He stops to take a deep breath. He's crying now. "Just know this: the team and me will always have an empty place because you're gone. Always."

He stands there holding the paper, then he goes back to take his seat with the Hornets. The team walked down the aisle together before the funeral began. I don't see Coach Perkins, though. I look around, then behind me—I think that's the coach sitting way in the back. I guess he couldn't find a place to park.

Pastor Burmeister talks about knowing Hargie from the time he was a baby.

"I baptized him right here. He had so much energy inside him. How he will be missed." Pastor Burmeister looks at Hargie's parents. "Michael and Dellia, we will gather around you—this church, this town. We will walk with you through this valley, through all of the shadows of this impossible loss. We will remember your boy, our boy. We will thank God for his life."

One by one, people stand to say, yes, we will support you.

We will remember.

◆ ◆ ◆

On the local news tonight, Coach Perkins stands by Hargie's poster in front of the Hornets' Nest.

"Hargie was like a son to me. He was a brilliant boy on and off the field." The coach shakes his head; his eyes fill with tears. "I wish it was me in the casket instead of him. Baseball has lost a superstar at every level—high school, college, and beyond, I'll tell you that. We're dedicating the rest of this season to Hargie Cantwell's memory. He was a gift to us all of excellence, strength, and fierce courage."

A blanket of sadness covers Hillcrest.

People light candles and put them in front of the Hornets' Nest.

People are quiet—on the bus, in the stores.

The middle school plants a tree by the baseball diamond in Hargie's memory.

At school, there are extra counselors around for kids to talk to about Hargie's death.

In English, we talk about how to construct an interesting opening sentence.

In Civilization class, we talk about ancient Greece.

In Science, we talk about what happens when atoms split.

At lunch, we talk about the rumors.

Did Hargie really have a heart attack, or . . .

Was he drunk, like some say?

On drugs?

Riding his bike so fast, his heart stopped? That can't happen, of course.

But everyone is trying to understand what happened in their own way.

The only good news this week comes from Dr. Dugan. Walt grins as he tells me. "Your blood looks good, blood pressure is just a little low, but Dr. Dugan doesn't want to change your meds yet. We'll see her and the transplant team next week." He high fives me.

Right now I'm at the public library that's between the high school and the middle school. It has a place to remember Hargie in one of the reading rooms—a long piece of paper hangs on the wall, and people write about their memories. There's a bench you can sit on to think about him.

I'm sitting on that bench, thinking about his fastball ripping across the plate.

I'm thinking about myself a little, too. I don't want to sound selfish—I mean, a kid has died. But I gave up a lot to come here, and now everything is changing.

I feel awful even thinking this way!

Franny and Benny walk into the room. Benny takes a green marker and carefully draws balloons with strings on the wall:

"Can you sign your name?" Franny asks him.

Benny shakes his head.

"Yes, you can. I've seen you do it lots of times."

"How many?" Benny asks.

Franny thinks about it. "Over a hundred and fifty-one times."

Benny writes:

B
e
nn
Y

Next to Benny's balloons, Franny writes:

Dear Hargie,
Thanks for showing me about working hard
and never giving up.
Your Fan 4ever,
Franny Engers

They see me now and sit with me on the bench. Benny kicks the back of the bench with his feet again and again. I wonder if he can understand about someone dying.

Benny whispers loudly, "Hargie died like Mufasa."

Franny nods. "That's right." She turns to me. "Benny's favorite movie is *The Lion King*."

Benny's face gets serious. "Scar is bad."

I nod. "Scar's a bad lion." Scar let Mufasa, the great lion ruler, die.

More bench kicking. "Forty-two," Benny says. "Jackie Robinson."

I smile. Jackie Robinson is my favorite ballplayer.

Franny looks at him. "How many hits did Jackie Robinson have, Benny?"

I know this. One thousand five hundred and eighteen.

"One five one eight," he says.

1,518. *This kid knows that?*

Franny asks, "How many home runs did Jackie Robinson have, Benny?"

I know that, too. One hundred thirty-seven.

Major bench kicking. "One three seven."

I'm looking at Benny. "That's very good."

"Very good," he says.

"Franny, that book you wanted on Canada is in."

A librarian tells her this; Franny goes to check it out. Benny and I wait for her.

I say, "Benny, how many bases did Jackie Robinson steal?"

He shakes his head, confused, and shouts, "No!"

Franny turns to look.

"No!" Benny says.

"Hey, I'm sorry. Wrong question!" I smile at him. "Forty-two."

That quiets him down for a minute. I don't mention that Mariano Rivera was the last player to wear the number.

Franny has her book; we go out the door. Benny decides to shout "No!" one more time. I try to change the subject. "Are you doing a report on Canada, Franny?"

She looks down. "No."

"My dad and I lived in Toronto one summer," I mention. "It's great there."

She doesn't say anything.

"Have you been to Canada, Franny? It's a big place." That was stupid. Everyone knows it's big.

She shouts, "I've never been, Jeremiah! Is that okay with you?"

"No!" Benny yells.

"I didn't mean to—"

"I don't want to talk about it!" Franny grabs Benny's hand and walks off.

I stand here watching them go.

What just happened?

Chapter
13

I'M LOOKING AT a map of Canada, trying to figure out why Franny got upset about this country. I am eating my third multigrain waffle with organic butter and real maple syrup. They are serious about their maple syrup in Canada. I love waffles so much that Walt had a toaster in my hospital room and we made them whenever. This was my push-back on Jell-O, which seemed to appear any time, day or night, even when I hung a NO JELL-O EVER sign on my bed.

But waffles! They fill the atmosphere with goodness. Nurses would come into my room, sniffing the air, and say, "That smells so good!"

"The downside of being a robot, Jerwal, is you can't eat waffles."

Jerwal cocks his head at me like a dog. It took forever to get his head movement right.

"I have no insight on Canada, Jerwal. Do you want to watch the eagle cam?"

Jerwal glows.

There are two eagle cams I follow. The baby eagles from the Nature Conservancy are doing really well. "Let's check in on the intact family."

I link to the streaming eagle site. Right now a parent eagle is sitting on the nest warming three eggs. Male and female eagles take turns doing nest duty, which I think is awesome. Yaff's mother mentioned this to Yaff's father, who said, "No kidding?" and went back to watching football and dropping peanut shells on the rug.

"I think the female eagle is on the nest, Jerwal."

Female eagles are a little bigger than the males. This one is pecking at the twigs, looking around, just content to sit there. You have to care about eagle details to get into this. It took Yaff a while to care. The fact that there was no audio drove him crazy. He kept screaming "This is boring!" when I first showed it to him, but then I explained that the babies in the eggs need protection, and the parent is showing a real dedication by not deserting the eggs or flying off to town to meet some friends after work and have a beer.

"Sometimes nature is quiet," I told him.

He got into it then and it was hard to pull him away.

Yaff has the heart of an eagle—no matter what comes at him, he deals with it.

I miss him. I scroll through my eagle pictures, find the best one of an eagle building a nest high up. I type, `I hope you're going to be busy while I'm gone,` and send it to him.

Whoosh.

Instant response: `I'm not cleaning my room till you come back.`

Smile. `How come?`

`Just seems right.`

`Later.`

`Yeah . . .`

Back to nature. The eagle mother sits on the big nest, watching, protecting—which is kind of what Walt did for me, except I'd already hatched when we met.

The babies should be pecking out of the shells in three weeks—that's what the nature people think. I have to set a timer when I watch, or I'll forget to do other things, like take my medicine.

Ping. I take two blue pills.

The mother eagle is rocking on the nest and opening her mouth like she's singing a raptor lullaby. Walt said when I was little and couldn't sleep, he'd sing me the Michigan fight song. He's such a bad singer, I think I went to sleep to protect myself.

The eagle cam helps you remember all the great people in your life who've been there for you.

◆　◆　◆

"I know you have genius in you." I tell Adler this as he drools. "It's not always clear right off. It's good you moved off the lawn. That's the first step to a deeper life."

I hold up a plastic bagel squeak toy. Right now we're working on get-the-bagel. I put it on our front porch. "Adler, get the bagel." Adler sniffs the air, doesn't move. "No." I say this sharply to remind him this is a command and I'm in charge. "Adler, get the bagel."

Adler trots over to the porch, takes the bagel in his mouth, and brings it over.

"Good dog!" I give him a serious rub on his neck. "Excellent dog!" Adler wants love more than snacks. "Let's do it again."

That's when Franny walks up. She doesn't look angry anymore, which is good, but no way am I mentioning Canada. "Hi, Franny. How are you doing?"

"Sub-okay."

"You must have known Hargie well."

"No. Bo did. He's . . . not talking to anybody."

Bo is sitting on the front porch of their house looking at his hands. Franny's mother jogs up the street, back from her run. She bends over, breathing hard.

Franny waves. "She's training for a half marathon," Franny tells me.

Mrs. Engers looks up. "It's conceivable I might die!"

"You look strong!" Franny shouts back.

"Ha!"

Bo just sits there.

I throw the bagel. It's a bad throw into Mrs. Prim's hedge. Adler, dog genius, can't find it.

I hear her old voice: "Well, I knew Hargie Cantwell, and I know his parents." Mrs. Prim is looking at us from over the hedge; she squeaks the bagel toy. "And I heard that when Coach Perkins went to pay the Cantwells a visit, Mike Cantwell wouldn't let him in the house. Matter of fact, he told him to get off the property!"

She throws the bagel on the ground. Adler runs to get it and brings it back to me.

"Good dog."

"Why would Mr. Cantwell do that?" Franny asks.

Mrs. Prim straightens up as much as she can. "I suppose like most things, time will tell."

WE DON'T HAVE to wait long for time to tell us.

COACH PERKINS ARRESTED
Winningest Coach in Hillcrest Hornets History
Accused of Giving Performance-Enhancing
Drugs to His Players

That news runs through Hillcrest like a wild horse you can't catch. Coach Perkins is out on bail the next day and shuts himself up in his house. The sheriff seals off the locker rooms at the high school and the stadium as part of the investigation.

A pile of Hornets hats are thrown in front of the stadium.

A TV reporter stands next to the pile and asks, "Did he do it?"

Did he?

Everyone is asking that.

"He did not do it!"

Chip Gunther stands in front of his sports store, furious, and points a finger at the TV camera.

"I know this man. I was head of the committee that brought him here. He'd give his life for his players. The thought, the misrepresentation, that he would do such a thing is wrong. You hear me? Wrong! This witch hunt better end. I'm inclined to think there are people in other places who want to see this man fall. Well, he's a winner and he's going to win this battle! I guarantee it!"

The Hornets cancel their next two games.

"I know Coach Perkins," Franny tells me. "I babysat for his kids. I made scrambled eggs in his kitchen!"

I don't know what to say to that.

Her eyes look so sad, like someone close to her has died.

I look for her at school—she's not there.

I look for her after school—she's not at the baseball diamond, and neither are the guys who always play.

Everyone has questions:

Are the Hornets taking steroids?

All of them?

Some of them?

When will we know?

So much is coming at us:

HORNETS SUSPENDED FROM LEAGUE PLAY
Will Six Championships Be Overturned?

And the biggest one yet:

DID STEROIDS KILL HARGIE CANTWELL?

"There is strong circumstantial evidence that steroids contributed to that young man's death," the prosecutor says. "A charge of manslaughter against this coach is warranted."

I'm on my front porch. I hear Franny's mother shout, "Bo, I can't imagine how you feel, but—"

"That's right, you can't!" Bo shouts back, and then he runs down Weldon Road. Mrs. Engers stands on her porch and watches him go.

Walt walks out holding the *Hillcrest Herald*. "This is tough stuff, my man."

It sure is. "What do you think about it, Walt?"

"If Perkins did it, if he decided to break the law and willfully put the kids under his care at risk like that . . . then I hope they throw the book at him."

I nod. "Coaches are supposed to protect their players, not hurt them."

"That's right." His face softens a little. "And listen, Jer, when things like this happen, focus on the people who are trying to do the right thing."

Chapter
15

I WANT TO be the kind of person who tries to do the right thing.

I'm in the cafeteria, in line with my tray, trying to make an informed decision.

I shake the cafeteria helper's hand. She's wearing plastic gloves. "I'm Jeremiah Lopper."

"Maude Denton."

"If I were your son, would you recommend the turkey loaf?"

Heads turn.

"If you were my ex-husband, I wouldn't recommend it."

Sky and Logo put their turkey loaf plates back.

I smile. "Thank you, ma'am. Lives have been spared."

That cracks her up. I move to the premade salad section—the safe ones covered with plastic wrap.

"Want to eat with us, Jeremiah?" It's Logo.

"Sure."

I follow them to their table, put my tray down, waste no time. "How's baseball practice going?"

"Aw, you know," Sky says.

"Nobody wants to play much," Logo adds.

"Why not?"

"Baseball's dying in this town."

I look him in the eye. "You don't look like you're dying."

Logo looks right back at me. "Steroid City. That's what people call Hillcrest now. My dad wants me out of baseball."

"Quit baseball?"

Sky leans forward. "There's nowhere to go, Jeremiah. We don't have enough guys to play in the league. The Hornets are suspended. We're dead."

I say, "I've thought a lot about dying."

They look at me strangely.

"And I talked to this guy once." He visited me in the hospital, actually, but they're not ready for that. "He played basketball and he told me about the best coach he ever had. The coach was in a wheelchair."

They sit up.

"His legs were dead, but everything else he had made up for it. He could make a basket from center court. You know what this coach told him?"

"What?" they say.

"He said, 'Sometimes when you think you're finished, you're just beginning.'" I smile at them. "Every time I want to give up, every time I think it's over, I think about that."

Franny sits at the table across from us, listening.

I eat my salad. "Can I ask you guys something? How good are you at baseball?"

I can see in their eyes they love the game.

"Sky can pitch fire," Logo says.

"Logo always tags them out at the plate," Sky adds.

I give them my eagle eye. "Do you know how many billions of people can't do that? Am I right, Franny?"

"You're right, Jeremiah."

I look at the guys. "You're going to let the thing you do so well die?"

"I don't know!" Sky shouts.

I lean forward. "You know what I think? If an adult doesn't know how to be responsible, if they mess things up for their kid or the kids around them, then that adult shouldn't have the power to keep ruining things for everyone."

I hear Franny take a deep breath.

Sky says, "We're dealing with a mess here."

"Did you make the mess?"

"No!" they say.

"How many guys could you get to practice with you?"

Logo thinks. "A few more. The triplets would come. Their mother wants them out of the house. If we get more, then will you . . . you know . . . come and help us get better?"

I stand up, check my phone. "I'm free tomorrow afternoon."

I'm free most every afternoon, but . . .

Sky says, "Okay. We'll get more players."

Logo stares at him. "By tomorrow?"

Sky crushes his juice carton. "The rest of the league has played three games."

"The league we're not in anymore," Logo adds.

"We need more players to get back in. Right?"

Logo looks down. "Right."

Sky stands. "You want to sit out the season or see if we can get a real team together?"

Logo coughs. "Can I get back to you on that?"

Sky throws pita bread at him.

Franny pinches his shoulder.

And, people, I feel the energy!

◆ ◆ ◆

"Jerwal, I'm home."

Swoop.

I'm in the kitchen. Jerwal rolls forward. "I want to tell you something." Jerwal waits. "I'm going to be a coach."

Jerwal keeps waiting.

"Is that good or what?"

That's Jerwal's code phrase to twirl around and beep.

I put my hand up, he puts his arm up, and we do a high five, although technically he only has three fingers.

A little robot dance.

Shoulders up, shoulders down.

Freeze.

Okay, Lopper. Are you going to play around or get serious?

I pull out my baseball from the moving box in the corner. I hold the ball, just hold it. Walt says if you hold a baseball long enough, it becomes part of you.

I get my glove and head outside. It's not like I'm a pitcher or anything. It's not like I can run right now.

But I can stand.

I stand in the middle of our lawn. My fingers form the two-seam fastball grip.

Lopper takes his time. This kid knows how to wait.

The batter's getting nervous.

Lopper squints into the sun.

His arm comes back; he lets strength move through his legs.

He releases the ball like a bullet.

The batter never sees it coming.

"Strike three!" the umpire calls.

Chapter

16

I HAVE FIVE baseball books open on the long black table. Walt is checking his phone. He does this day and night, and probably while he sleeps. I've been reading about what it means to be a winner. Everyone seems to agree on this: You've got to think like one to be one. You've got to let it fill your head.

But is winning really everything? If you can only be satisfied when you win, I'm not sure you'll be a good ballplayer.

Walt is typing away on his computer. SARB is on the table going around in a circle.

"What makes people good at baseball, Walt?"

His eyes don't leave the screen. "Skill."

Actually, that's deeper than it sounds.

"I want to help this team."

"They've got to do the drills. Focus on the fundamentals. Catching, throwing, pitching, hitting. Over and over."

That makes sense.

"Take pitchers." Walt pushes back from the screen. "Sometimes they think the whole game's on their backs. In some ways it is. But they don't take their time to throw. They don't play the psych-out game they should to get the batter nervous."

I'm taking notes. "That's good, Walt."

Walt gets that Baseball Is Life look in his eyes. He's talking to me, but in his head he's back in high school playing ball.

"When you're out there, Jer, and you smell the grass, you feel the ball in your hand, you hear the crack of the bat, you feel your legs pumping to get around the bases, your heart is pounding, and they're cheering, and you slide into home—you don't even think about it, you just slide because that's what makes the play. You do it. You do what makes the play."

"Okay," I say. "That's good."

He leans back. "You're gonna help them, huh?"

"Yeah."

Walt nods. "Remember, take it easy at first. Change one thing at a time. That's what people can handle."

"Is it like that with robots?"

"They're programmed. They do what they're told." He sighs. "Unless there's a bug in the system."

He throws SARB on the floor. SARB goes backward.

"No, no, no!" Walt says.

◆ ◆ ◆

I have to miss the first two periods of school because I have an appointment with my new cardiology team.

Walt and I are sitting in Dr. Dugan's office. Walt drops his phone when she walks in.

"You do that a lot," she mentions.

Walt mutters, "Sorry."

Two men in white coats follow her, Dr. Paul and Dr. Bonano.

"We're very encouraged about your blood work, Jeremiah. And your monitor readings are pretty good, considering. We're going to make a small adjustment in your medication that will make you feel better, but first,

I want to do a biopsy. Dr. Bonano will handle that."

I've had a lot of those—especially the first year after my transplant. It's how they double-check to see if there are any signs your body is rejecting the new heart. Believe me—I want to keep this heart!

"Low blood pressure can zap energy," she says.

I know that. I've gotten used to being tired.

Dr. Dugan closes the folder and leans forward. I can see her freckles and her blue eyes. She says to me, "So now, tests and numbers aside, how are you doing?"

"I want to play baseball."

"Me too," says Dr. Paul. "Center field for the Yankees." Everyone laughs.

Dr. Dugan looks at me and waits. I raise my right hand that's holding the baseball. "I know I can't, but I want to."

"You're carrying a baseball around with you?"

I slept with it, actually. I kept rolling over on it and waking up, but that's not the point.

"It helps me." That's the point.

"Are you playing?" she asks.

"No."

"Can you play catch?"

I look to Walt, who says, "We used to; we haven't done that for—"

I sit up straight. "I can play catch."

"And if you miss the ball," Dr. Dugan says, "how do you get it?"

I know this is a trick question. The normal answer is, I run after it, scoop it up, and do a hop and a skip and a fierce throw to Walt using everything I've got.

I don't say that.

"I walk slowly like a snail, pick it up, walk slowly back, and throw it to Walt."

She laughs. Walt does, too, and drops his phone.

Dr. Dugan writes something on a pad and hands it to me. "Give this to the principal at your school. Doctor's orders."

I look at the "prescription."

Please allow Jeremiah Lopper to carry his baseball around school. It's for physical therapy.

Sarah M. Dugan, MD

She stands up. "Jeremiah, you have the kind of vision that gives you great energy for living. I don't want to hold you back, but there are limitations to your life right now. Listen to me—when you're tired, don't ignore it. Cut back."

Walt looks at me. "I will," I tell her.

She smiles. "But I feel very strongly that the two of you need to start playing catch."

◆ ◆ ◆

I want to play catch immediately, but I have to go to school.

I walk into Hillcrest Middle School holding the ball in the two-seam fastball grip. I hand Mr. Hazard the note from Dr. Dugan.

"I need to hold this in school, sir. It won't interfere with my work, I promise."

Mr. Hazard looks at the baseball, at the note.

"It's a big thing for me, sir."

"All right, Jeremiah."

I walk past Sky and Logo, toss my ball up in the air, catch it, and keep walking.

"See you later, Jeremiah!"

"Later."

I hold it in my left hand during my Civilization class because I have to take notes. Mr. Aronson is telling us about lies, deception, and intense treachery in ancient Greece.

"Mythology is full of nastiness," he says. "Gods using their powers to get whatever they want, no matter the cost."

A friend of Franny's raises her hand. "Did they have steroids back then?"

The class laughs.

"Actually, they sort of did. They had their own form of PEDs—performance-enhancing drugs. Athletes would eat things that we would find disturbing because it enhanced performance. Winning at all costs was valued by their society." He takes off his glasses and looks at us. "Is it valued in our society?"

That gets us going. Lots of hands go up, mine included. At the end of class we take a vote.

Are cheating, lying, and breaking laws to win acceptable in America?

Acceptable: 7

Unsure: 3

Not acceptable: 16

Mr. Aronson puts our results on the wall outside his classroom.

He says, "The sixth graders of Ancient Civilization class have spoken."

Will anyone listen, I wonder?

Chapter 17

LOGO AND SKY actually found nine players.

I've spent an hour watching them play, although two of them—Casey and a big kid named Benchant— tell me they're not sure their parents will let them be on the team. Casey can field and pitch, but he can't pitch as well as Sky. Benchant could be an awesome hitter if he learns to focus.

The triplets, the Oxley brothers, are in the outfield. They keep running into one another, and I just want to shout, "Play your positions!"

I'm taking it in, taking notes.

"All right," I say. "Here it is." The team looks at me. "I'm seeing things that will keep me up at night! You've got attitude, but not discipline. I'm seeing good players not trying hard, I'm seeing throws that aren't close to the bases. Why is this?"

The team looks down.

"'Cause you know what? Some of you guys are good, and the rest of you can get good, but you've got to want it."

Franny and Benny walk to the side of the field and sit down.

I say, "It's all about the three Ws. Are you ready?"

The guys shrug.

"Ready!" Benny shouts.

"Want, work, wow," I tell them.

They don't get that.

"You've got to want to do this. You've got to work hard to get there. You've got to push for the wow in your playing. Say it."

Alex Oxley raises his hand. "Which part?"

"Wow!" Benny shouts.

I repeat the three Ws.

Want. Work. Wow.

We say it over and over until they get it.

Benny is shouting it out, even when we stop.

The big guy, Benchant, steps forward like he hates the whole world. "How do you know this, Lopper?"

"I study the game."

Benchant's in my face. "How come you don't play?"

"'Cause I can't."

"Why not?"

I push back. "Because I've got a weak heart."

Everyone is quiet.

Now they know.

"Come on." Terrell throws the ball to Benchant.

I shout, "That's the way."

I sit with Franny and Benny. Benny's got a board out and is moving baseball players around the diamond. "Want, work, wow," he says.

Benny keeps his eye on the field, then his board.

I want to ask him, *What do you see, Benny?*

Franny is wearing a baseball glove. I point to it.

"This means nothing, Jeremiah."

"Did you play?"

She shrugs.

"I miss playing," I tell her.

She nods. "But you don't have a weak heart, Jeremiah."

"I had to have an operation and—"

Franny shakes her head. "I mean the other kind of heart. That one in you is strong."

You don't know what you just said to me, Franny.

◆ ◆ ◆

"Just see it, Jer," Walt reminds me. "Remember, it's all that you see."

"It" is the baseball.

Walt is throwing easy to me, like I'm six years old. I decide not to mention this. I've only missed a couple of throws.

I toss one in the air that he has to run for. Walt groans and reaches for it. He gets it. *Just* gets it. He grins at me, and I grin back.

He throws it a little left so I have to reach. I miss that one. I do my snail walk to get it.

"I'm planning on running one of these days, Walt!" I throw long. He bobbles it, but doesn't drop it.

We're both rusty, but this is so excellent. You don't need to think much when you play catch; you just keep your eye on the ball, follow the rhythm, and let everything else go.

Throw.

Catch.

Throw.

Catch

Focus.

We go for twenty-two minutes, then Walt says we should stop.

"Why?" I can keep going.

"We're not overdoing."

I know not to fight this. "It was good, Walt."

"It was, Jer."

He taught me to catch a ball when I was three and a half. I'd rather play catch with Walt than go to a World Series game.

Okay, maybe not that, but you get the idea.

Chapter

18

"JEREMIAH, HOW ARE you doing?" Dr. Bonano asks.

"Okay." I'm lying on a table.

"I'm guiding the catheter now."

That's a thin tube that he placed in my vein. It's on its way to my heart.

Welcome to my biopsy.

"You with me?"

"Uh-huh . . ." I feel dopey from the medicine they gave me.

"Lie still."

A nurse checks a machine. "All right now . . ." Dr. Bonano is checking another screen. "You know how this goes. I'm going to remove a few little pieces from your heart muscle."

Sorry, Alice.

"Here we go, Jeremiah." I try not to picture chunks of my heart being snipped. "And another one . . ."

I close my eyes. I feel pressure where they put the tube in. My mouth is dry. Lying still isn't the easiest thing during a biopsy.

"And one more piece for good measure."

"Breathe slowly," the nurse tells me.

I do. In and out . . . nice and slow . . .

I've had so many biopsies.

"Okay, Jeremiah, you're doing great. I'm going to bring the catheter out now."

I can see the moving picture of this on the screen.

Okay, Alice, you're looking great. Looking strong.

Now *this* would make a great science fair project!

"Almost done, my friend."

"You're doing fine," the nurse says.

I lie so still. I just want it to be over.

The anesthesiologist nods and says, "We are A-okay."

On the screen I see my heart inside my chest, beating away.

This biopsy is to make sure my new heart is behaving itself.

The tube is out now. The nurse rubs my hand. "Nice job."

I nod. I get a bandage, then Walt comes in. We've been through this a lot, me and my dad.

"Hey, pal."

"Hey." I try to clear my head. "How are the . . . Reds doing against . . . um . . . ?"

"LA?" Walt laughs. "Do you ever not think about baseball?"

I shake my head.

"So how are they doing against LA?" Dr. Bonano wants to know.

Walt describes the game like an announcer. He knows I don't want to miss a thing. He knows just about everything about me, except for those first nine months.

◆ ◆ ◆

I'm home and a little sore—just a little. I don't remember when they said we'd get the results. I hate waiting, but actually, I'm pretty good at it.

Kids say things like, "I'm waiting for my mother."

"I'm waiting for my sister to get out of the bathroom."

"I'm waiting to see what grade I got on the test."

That's not real waiting.

Real waiting is long and hard, like waiting eleven months and seventeen days to see if you'll get a donor heart so you can keep living.

All that waiting with nothing happening, then everything happens faster than you can imagine so the donor heart stays strong.

I know about waiting.

Chapter
19

I AM NOT supposed to overdo. I am supposed to cut back when I'm tired.

But I would like to mention that baseball takes time and energy. Developing talent in people does, too. It isn't easy. You have to put yourself out there, hoping like crazy you'll get a break. Hoping sucks up a lot of energy. People don't think about that.

We have ten players now. Donald Mole wants to play. The problem is Donald Mole can't hit, run, catch, or field.

But if we get one more player, just one, then Mr. Hazard says the Lincoln Middle School Tornadoes will play us tomorrow. This is huge, but as I emphasized to Walt, this is not overdoing!

The problem is, we can't find that eleventh player.

I look at Franny, who says, "I don't know anyone."

"But do you play?"

"No."

So we practice drills and footwork and running and hitting. We practice catching on the run, how to stand at the plate, how not to drop the ball.

"You hold on to it like it's a wad of money," I tell them. "And I want you to hustle. On and off the field. Your mother tells you to do the dishes? You do it with energy! Get excited. And bring it out on the field every day!"

I tell Donald, "Picture in your mind where you want that ball to go when you hit it."

"I can't," he says. At least he's honest.

"Where would you like it to go, Donald?"

He thinks hard. "Between the second baseman and the shortstop in Yankee Stadium."

"Keep thinking big, Donald." I turn to the team. "Does anyone know one more player?"

Donald Mole raises his hand. "I know lots of players, but they don't want to play."

"Why not?"

"They don't understand what's happening here," he says quietly.

I wish I could teach you to play, Donald. You've

got the heart, but absolutely no talent.

I end practice on this: "If you can find anybody for tomorrow, bring them."

Danny Lopez says, "The Tornadoes will kill us."

Sky says, "Not playing is killing us more."

"We're dead either way." That's Logo.

"No death allowed," I tell them. "Nobody's out there alone. We're a team. Remember?" I read the roster. "We've got Sky pitching, Casey as relief pitcher, Logo catching, Benchant on first base, Donald on second, Danny Lopez on third, the Oxleys in the outfield." The triplets cheer. "Terrell Younger—shortstop." *We hope and pray Terrell will cover second base, too.* "Good work today."

The team heads home. I stand alone on the field and look at the tree the school planted in Hargie's memory. It's surrounded by a little fence to protect it because (for lack of a better garden explanation) it's a baby.

I'd like to put a protective fence around my guys. They won't need it forever, but just for a little while. I think of an eagle's nest that's built to last—high up in a tree to avoid predators. It's a condo. It's a fort.

I think of all the coaches in history who stood on their fields hoping their teams wouldn't embarrass themselves. There are so many great coaches out there. Why did Hillcrest get stuck with two such bad ones?

I look at the huge baseball bat glistening on the little hill.

"Jeremiah!" Mr. Hazard walks toward me, waving. "I've spoken to the coach of the Tornadoes. They have two injured players and are down to ten, like us. They agreed to play a game tomorrow. What do you think?"

I shake his hand. "Mr. Hazard, I don't know if we can win, but we're going to play our best."

"I like that attitude, Jeremiah!"

"We've been focusing on hustle, sir."

"Keep it up!"

And he's off. I walk across the street and take out my phone. There's a message from Walt.

```
Your biopsy results came back
normal, Jer. You don't need the
monitor.
```

I knew it! I feel totally free! I love being normal—I mean, medically normal.

I don't know how to contact all the players, but the ones I can get this:

Tomorrow it begins.

10 players. 7 innings.

Be there with your best and stop the
Tornadoes.

Pass it on.

Chapter
20

I'M IN CIVILIZATION class with Mr. Aronson, and doing everything I can to pay attention. The ancient Greeks started the Olympics and were big on sports and competition, so I think they would appreciate that I can't give this my best right now.

I have to save that for baseball!

Mr. Aronson writes *The tragic flaw* on the board. He explains, "This is important to understand. What does *tragic* mean?"

Franny raises her hand. "Something awful and sad."

"That's right."

He's got my attention.

"What's a flaw?" he asks us.

No one says anything.

"Class . . . ?" He holds up a glass. "Right here"—he points to the rim—"is a crack. It's hard to see. Eventually it will get worse and probably cause the glass to break." He smiles. "So what's a flaw?"

I raise my hand. "It's a defect that makes something weak."

"That's right. The Greeks understood about defects in the human heart. They wrote stories about people and gods who had great strengths, but their weakness, their flaw, was so great, it caused their downfall."

On the board, Mr. Aronson writes:

PRIDE

ANGER

LOVE OF MONEY

EXCESSIVE LOYALTY

"These were some of the flaws explored in Greek tragedy. Tonight I want you to read the story of Achilles, the greatest warrior in the ancient world. Then fill out his report card." He smiles.

We look at one another. *Report card?*

The bell rings.

"Go forth," Mr. Aronson tells us. "Do no harm."

He always ends class that way. I head for the field.

Hearts sure are complicated.

◆ ◆ ◆

I'm not sure how the ancient Greeks would feel about what I need to say to the team. I've got exactly forty-five minutes to get them game-ready.

"Guys, I've been thinking." I'm chewing gum, which I don't usually do, but baseball players chew gum constantly, and their managers chew gum like it's the only thing keeping them from biting somebody. I hand out gum to the team.

"Chew," I say. "Really hard." They start chewing. "Wad it up in your cheek. Go for it. You want more?" A couple of guys take another stick.

"What are we doing?" Terrell asks.

I'm not sure they're ready for this. "You're looking like serious ballplayers."

They chew harder and spit on the ground.

"Yeah!" I say.

More spitting.

"There it is," I say. "Awesome."

More chewing.

"I'm not saying skill isn't important in baseball—that takes time to develop, but something you can do in this game could open the door to big things."

"Spitting?" Logo asks.

I'm going to have to lead them. "It's not just the spitting; it's what the spitting means. It means you're tough." All of them spit. I back up a little. "And when you feel tough, you look different, you play different. Name me one top ball team that doesn't chew gum and spit."

They can't do it.

"See?" I say. "We'll work on the game, but this is first."

I spit.

They spit.

"You guys are kind of scary when you do that."

They stand a little taller, they nod—a tough nod. A couple of them scratch, too, which is a good thing to add, but I don't want to get too complicated.

The Tornadoes walk onto the field. Mr. Darko, Hillcrest Middle School's soccer coach, runs over. He's our official school-sponsored adult.

Casey asks, "What if they chew and spit?"

"You do it better."

"Yeah. Okay."

Mr. Darko looks confused. "I think I missed something."

"We're getting in the zone, sir."

My guys chew hard and spit like all-stars. Mr. Darko jumps back.

The Tornadoes don't have gum. Too bad.

"Aw right!" I shout. "Let's play ball!"

"I don't know if I can pitch and chew," Sky mentions.

"You can do it." I'm clapping to get them to hustle.

"We have mouth guards, Jeremiah."

"Work it out. You're ballplayers!"

◆ ◆ ◆

We didn't win, but we didn't look that bad losing. And we had four fierce parents to cheer us on.

The final score: 4–1. That's respectable for a first game. On my notepad I write, MAXIMUM IMPACT. That's what this team needs to have in a short period of time. It would be nice if we had another game to play.

I'm clapping. "Keep the energy up, keep the focus. Who are we?"

"The Muskrats!" they shout.

Man. Who picked that name?

I raise my fist. "We are baseball in Hillcrest!"

Big cheers.

Then the reality of that sets in.

Chapter

21

ACHILLES, LET ME tell you, had issues.

I give him an A+ on the battlefield, but an F in Taking Advice, Handling Insults, and Being a Team Player. He gets a big "Needs work" on Anger Management, too. My recommendation is that Achilles's parents, Thetis and Peleus, come in immediately for a teacher's conference, although this could be tense because Thetis is a sea nymph and can morph into different shapes. I suspect his mother is a big part of the problem.

A lot of people in Hillcrest get a "Needs work" in Anger Management. Walt says nobody thinks clearly when they're mad. You should lock yourself in a room and not make any decisions until you're calmer.

Everywhere, the news is bad, and hardly anyone is taking it calmly.

STEROID USE RAMPANT AMONG HILLCREST HORNETS, INVESTIGATION SHOWS

6 PLAYERS OUT OF 15 TEST POSITIVE FOR STEROID USE

I show it to Walt. His face gets stiff.

I hold my baseball so tight, my arm hurts.

"The players are under a doctor's care," says the sheriff.

"We can only hope and pray there will not be permanent damage to these young athletes," says Pastor Burmeister of Peaceful Lutheran Church.

The Hornets who tested positive for steroids have a lawyer. She says, "My clients, these fine young athletes, didn't know what the coach was giving them. He assured them they were taking vitamins."

Coach Perkins has two lawyers. One of them says, "We are confident that the truth will come out and that Delmar Perkins's innocence will be upheld." The other lawyer says, "Coach Perkins loves his players more than he loves himself."

The lawyer for the high school says, "This is a tragedy at many levels, and Hillcrest High School is addressing it with speed, accountability, and compassion."

The media loves this story.

"In the little town of Hillcrest, nestled in Ohio's

western hills, there was a dark secret, so dark that a boy with exceptional promise is now dead, and one of the country's most respected high school baseball programs has been suspended, the coach arrested, the town left grappling with a big question: Who are we now?"

Suspended.

Canceled.

Embarrassed.

The town welcome sign about pushing to be the best is taken down. The baseball bat statue on the hill feels like it shouldn't be there.

Shame on you.

That's what one article said. The shame was on us and it stuck, like stepping in dog doo—even if you scrape it off, there's still the smell.

Words have such power.

We're trying to hustle during baseball practice to find the energy, but it's hard to do that when so much around you says you're a fake.

But there's one person who isn't upset by any of this. He can't understand steroids and cheating and losing your reputation. But Benny Lewis thinks our team and our town are great.

He can't wait to see us play. He shouts "Yay!" and "Good catch!" even when it isn't a good one.

For three days, Benny doesn't come to practice because he has to have tests at his doctor's office. And for three days, it isn't the same. Even Benchant misses him.

"The little guy's okay, right?"

"He's coming tomorrow," Franny tells us. But Benny gets strep throat. He has to stay home.

And it feels to me like the town is getting weaker. I think Hillcrest needs a heart transplant. But before you can put the new heart in, you have to take the old heart out.

I'm thinking about this while Walt wraps a sheet halfway around me and fastens it at the shoulder. I'm playing Aristotle in Think About It Day at my school. One day a month a kid dresses up like a famous dead person and walks around school saying things that are supposed to make everyone think differently. Aristotle is a major ancient Greek who thought hard about everything.

I adjust the fake beard Mr. Aronson gave me to wear. Walt and I look in the mirror together—two guys with beards.

"I still don't look like you, Walt."

"The sheet doesn't help, Jer."

Mr. Aronson and I reworked some of Aristotle's sayings so kids could get the general idea and not be bored into oblivion. Jerwal rolls into the room and stops. I raise my right arm, let my voice go deep.

"Excellence is formed in a person who works at being excellent."

Jerwal beeps.

"I like that." Walt scoops up SARB, who is stuck in the corner.

I scratch under my beard and head toward the door. It's not easy walking in a sheet.

◆　◆　◆

Kids at school don't connect to the sheet right off, and lots of them laugh when I stop in the hall, raise my arm, and say major things.

"Dignity does not come by having honors, but by deserving them."

"All people are alike when they sleep."

In the cafeteria, I shout: "Happiness rocks!" That's a very loose translation, but kids totally get the concept.

Benchant pulls my beard. Logo calls out, "Way to

go, Big A!" I nod wisely and try not to trip on my sheet.

Mr. Aronson is beyond happy. "We're shooting energy through this school. Good job, Jeremiah."

I feel the energy building. Donald Mole shows up to practice with two more players, Handro Corea and Roy Nader.

"Handro should play second base," Donald tells me.

"But you're on second."

"He's better."

Handro runs on the field and starts throwing and catching. He's so much better. Roy picks up a bat and Sky pitches to him. He's got a power swing.

"Okay, Donald, you and Roy are utility players. That means you'll play different positions as we need you." I slap his shoulder. "It's awesome what you did."

"I want us to win."

We've now got twelve guys!

A reporter from out of town comes to watch us practice. He has a little mustache and a lot of snark. "So what do you kids think of baseball now?"

Everyone looks to me. I say, "Was it baseball that did this, sir, or people?"

He has a fake smile. "So will you be playing baseball in school even after all that's happened?"

Terrell steps up. "As you can see, mister, we are playing baseball after all that's happened! And we're going to keep playing it."

"Why?" the reporter demands.

Terrell points a finger at him. "Because my grandpa always told me, giving up is stupid."

The reporter sits there.

"You should write down what he said," I tell the man.

"What's the name of your team?"

"The Muskrats." Terrell says it strong.

The reporter turns to me. "And you are . . . ?"

"He's our coach," Donald says.

"Really? Do you Muskrats have a captain?"

We hadn't thought about that. But most of the players look to Terrell, then back at me. "It's Terrell if he'll do it," I say.

A big cheer goes up. Terrell's smiling. If we ever get new uniforms, maybe we should have GIVING UP IS STUPID written on the backs of our jerseys.

There's another message going around town: HONK IF YOU LOVE BASEBALL.

I didn't have anything to honk when I first saw it, so I shouted, "Yes!" I expected to hear a lot of honking, but there wasn't much.

I wonder what happened to all the people who loved it? I wonder about the other people—the ones who say:

What's the big deal about steroids?

You think this is only happening in Hillcrest?

So many people want that edge to WIN.

WIN.

WIN.

But in the middle of all this, another voice rises— it's a real one, too. She stands on the high school steps with her husband and her son, Mac Rooney, who was a big Hornets star. Mac Rooney's mother gives motherhood a gold star.

"I don't know how the other parents are feeling," she begins. "But I'm feeling that we're the lucky ones. We still have our sons. Michael and Dellia Cantwell lost their boy, Hargie. I, for one, want to know the truth about what happened. I want to understand what trust was broken, I want to understand what my son was exposed to, what he knew and didn't know. I want us all to stop running from this ugly thing and look at what's at stake here! If we ever needed truth in this town, we need it now."

Mac Rooney is standing next to his mother when she says it and applauding louder than anyone.

Then Mr. Aronson gives us the best homework assignment. "What's an example of a tragic flaw in our world today? Write a paragraph about that."

I haven't finished my paragraph about Coach Perkins, but here's what I've got so far.

His love for winning was his downfall. It became more important than being honest and being responsible to his players and to the sport. I really like this sentence: *Finally, when it comes down to it, a coach is responsible for the health and safety of his players.*

I actually call Aunt Charity and read it to her.

"Well done," she says. "You're getting quite an education in that place." And she doesn't ask if I've had a bowel movement!

Of course, I get off the phone before she can.

I ask Franny who she wrote about. At first she doesn't want to tell me. Remembering Canada, I let it be. But later in the day, she comes up to me.

"Promise you won't tell."

"I promise."

She stands there quietly. "I wrote about my dad."

Chapter
22

I HAVE A million questions I want to ask Franny about her dad, but everything says *Don't*.

I'm trying to show Jerwal how to pick up a garbage bag. I'm live-streaming this to Yaff, but Jerwal's not getting it.

"When you learn this, Jerwal, you can begin to clean my room," I explain. "Won't that be great?"

"Then you can clean my room," Yaff tells him.

Jerwal shuts down at that, except for the blinking light in his eyes.

"We'll talk about this later, Jerwal."

Yaff sends me pictures of the science fair. Our tables were supposed to have been next to each other. "They put Lanie Costrider next to me! She won first prize with 'How We Can Save the Ozone Layer.' But I got more traffic."

Yaff brought his gerbil, Brucie, to the fair. He built a maze for him to follow and tested how fast Brucie went through it. He changed the treats and colors so you could see what got Brucie moving and what made him stop. Yaff got awarded a SCIENCE IS FUN ribbon for his project. He hung the ribbon over the maze to show off, but Brucie got hold of it and started shredding it.

"When are you coming back?" Yaff asks.

I sigh. "I'm not sure."

"So, see you pretty soon, Eagle Man."

"Yeah . . . pretty soon . . ."

I don't know how long I've got to rescue baseball.

And here's the worst part: I don't want to go back. I like my life in St. Louis, and I really miss Yaff—but wait! I can't think this way!

Head in the game, Lopper.

Across the street, Bo is lugging an old suitcase from the garage. Then he carries out a broken rocking horse. Franny runs out of the house.

"No! Not the horse. That's mine."

Bo puts the horse down. It doesn't rock; it flops over. He shakes his head. "It's dead, Franny!"

"It's not dead!" she yells.

El Grande stands up slowly and says something to

them I can't hear. Now El Grande is walking across the street toward me. Adler follows him. "Son, I want to talk to you."

"Yes, sir."

He looks at Jerwal, whose robot eyes glow. El Grande shakes his head. "I feel like I'm in a space movie."

"It's just everyday robotics."

He unfolds the *Hillcrest Herald*. "I've heard from people on both sides about baseball at the middle school. I don't know if you've seen this yet."

IS BASEBALL HISTORY IN HILLCREST?

I feel my heart racing.

I'm getting sick of this!

Chill, Alice!

"We need a break here! How can we keep playing when nobody cares?" I flop down on the porch steps and put my head in my hands.

Jerwal beeps. El Grande lowers himself on a step.

"I figured you'd feel that way, and I came to tell you something. You know what blinders do for a horse when it's running a race?"

"I think they keep the horse from looking around at other things."

"That's right. And I'm inclined to think you need to figure out a way to tell the team about keeping their eyes away from all these voices that are squawking and discouraging everybody. You've got a team to build and a job to do. It doesn't matter what the other people say."

I look at a crack in the step. "That's good, sir."

"When I played ball, my coach always told me, 'Ellis, you've got to play your game.' I was never sure what my game was, to tell the truth, until one day we were behind twelve runs—it was the eighth inning and hotter than a pizza oven outside. Any fans we had were long gone. I hated baseball that day, I hated my life, and I didn't think I had a blasted thing left to give. But I did."

I look up. "What was it?"

"Well, I laughed. Good and long."

"You laughed?"

"That's right. I laughed because I decided to play the last part of a losing game the best I'd ever played. I went on to get two home runs and stopped three guys from scoring."

"Did you win?"

"I sure did. My team lost bad. But I won. You get what I'm saying?"

I sit there grinning. "I get it. Thank you."

It takes him a while to stand up. "I hate to say something so insightful and then have such trouble taking my leave."

"You don't have to leave, sir."

"Tell you what, now that we're friends, you can call me Coach or El Grande, but let's be done with sir."

I grin. "El Grande—definitely."

Jerwal beeps.

El Grande looks at my robot. "You're going to take some getting used to."

There should be special movie music when El Grande walks back across the street to his house.

"We've been visited by greatness, Jerwal."

I can't wait to talk to the team.

I wish I was about ten years older, but you don't always get what you want.

Chapter

23

ON THE LOCAL news, Rabbi Tova is mad as anything and she's not taking it anymore.

She stands on the steps of Town Hall with half her congregation and shouts, "Is baseball history in Hillcrest? If you mean the kind of baseball that uses steroids to cheat and win and harm young players, then, yes indeed, it is history here!"

Walt and I clap at that and turn on the Reds game. We both have work to do, but it's good to have a baseball game happening in the background. It gives you comfort, except for the commercials.

I'm all for comfort right now. The new medicine Dr. Dugan gave me has a side effect—dry mouth. I feel like I'm in the desert. Walt says she's going to change the medication again to see if it makes me feel better.

Better is good; getting worse is not acceptable. We're picking up the pills tomorrow. "I asked her about side effects, Jer."

"And . . . ?"

"She said you might urinate more in the beginning."

"Come on! I hate that."

"Sorry, pal. Maybe you won't."

I probably will, but I can't think about that now. Tomorrow will be my first big speech to the team, and it's got to be right. Mr. Hazard got us a game in two days against the Myerson Middle School Bolts. I spread out my coaching books for inspiration.

There are speeches coaches give in the middle of a game when their team is losing: *You're better than this! Remember that! I know what you can do!*

That's not the kind of speech I need.

There are speeches coaches give near the end of a game when their team is losing: *When you look in the mirror tomorrow, will you be able to say "I did everything I could to win"?*

Will you?

I'm going to have to write my own.

From the heart, Alice.

◆ ◆ ◆

I practice the speech in front of Jerwal, who moves back and forth.

I practice it in front of Adler, who really wants to play get-the-bagel.

All during school I think about it. It's going to be a big moment.

After school when the guys come on the field, Benchant walks up to me.

"I'm not sure I can stay on the team, Lopper."

"Why not?"

He shrugs.

Then Casey says he's not sure he can keep playing, either. We can't lose our reliever!

This is bleak!

We go through some fundamental drills. Danny Lopez, our third baseman, isn't here. So I adjust . . .

"Donald, you're on third." He half runs over there. We do the ground ball drill. We do the fly ball drill. Donald misses every time. He even drops the ball Terrell hands to him.

There's no hustle on this field, except from Terrell.

I can't stand it anymore. I wave my arms for them to stop. "You're not the same team! What happened?"

They look down.

Handro steps forward. "We're going to get killed tomorrow, Jeremiah. Myerson is seriously good. Man, we are not ready."

I don't know what to do. "Is that how the rest of you feel?"

Logo and the Oxleys nod.

"So, what would make you feel ready?"

Sky laughs. "A couple of wins."

This feels like a Magellan moment, when people were telling him it was impossible to circle the globe because there was no globe and he'd better wake up to reality.

I cross my arms like coaches do. "All I can tell you is what I know. Winning isn't just about who gets the most runs—that's not the point."

Donald Mole is leaning on his bat, listening like I've got the secret to the universe.

This was not the speech I planned at all. "Winning," I tell them, "is deciding you're not going to quit."

They look at one another.

"You've got to do the hard work and decide you're going to keep at it, bit by bit, no matter how tough it gets."

Now Benchant looks straight at me.

"Here's the word we kill here and now," I tell them. The guys wait for the word, just like I waited for it when Walt told me this in the hospital. *"Quitter."* I kick the sand. "That's dead to us. We destroy it." I stomp my foot like I'm squishing a bug.

Terrell is looking around at the faces; he looks back at me and nods. He's not quitting.

I stare at them. "So what are you not going to be?"

"Quitters!" they say.

"I want you to write it down. 'I'm not a quitter.'"

Benchant raises his hand. "I don't have any paper."

"Do it when you get home! Write it down every day. And next to it, write 'I'm a winner.'"

Benchant says, "How come you know this, Lopper?"

I learned it when I got sick and I thought I was going to die, and I was too sick to care, but Walt told me. He put courage in me.

I say, "I play the game in my head. I picture all the things that can go wrong and I see myself stepping over them and getting it right."

Benchant glares at me.

"You know what, Benchant? Glare at the pitcher just like that. It's awesome."

That throws him. "It is?"

"Positively awesome. Like a secret weapon." I slap him on the back.

He smiles a little. "You think?"

I smile back. "I know. And that's for all of you. Attitude on the field. I want you to practice that. Game faces on."

They get serious.

"Okay," I shout. "Who are we?"

"The Muskrats!" they yell back.

We need to do something about that name.

❖ ❖ ❖

Danny comes late to practice. I give him a shorter version of the speech. "You have to play tomorrow," I tell him. "We need you."

"I'll be there."

I give Franny the entire speech, and she says, "Where did you learn to think like that?"

"My dad mostly."

Franny looks down. "I learned the exact opposite from my dad."

"Where is your father?" I ask.

She doesn't answer.

I don't push. "You're coming tomorrow, right? We need loyal, cheering fans."

"Benny and I will be there."

"It's nice you take care of him."

"Benny has a special way of looking at the world. And believe me, Jeremiah, after everything . . ." She stops. "It's the least I can do."

What does that mean, Franny?

And she walks into her house.

Chapter
24

"WE'RE GOING TO cheer for our team, Benny."

Franny says this, and Benny shouts, "Yay!"

"Louder, Benny Man," says Sky.

Benny screams it louder.

"You're our mascot," Terrell tells him.

Benny looks confused. He doesn't understand *mascot*.

Our bus pulls up to Myerson Middle School. Mr. Darko, the soccer coach, has been assigned to us permanently. He doesn't say anything encouraging; he just claps and says, "Okay now, okay."

Out the window, I see Walt parking his car. I asked him to come to the game. I know he had to reschedule a lot to be here. Four Hillcrest mothers are holding up a GO, MUSKRATS! sign and cheering as our bus pulls up.

Benny jumps off, shouting "Yay!" The team follows.

The mothers sit in the bleachers. Walt walks with us to the field. And that's when we hear it.

We look at one another.

At the crowd.

Is that about us?

It is.

We're getting booed. Good and loud.

I've never been booed before.

The team freezes.

I make the mistake of looking at the people booing. They seem to enjoy it.

The Hillcrest mothers are angry.

"Cheaters!" someone shouts.

Benny backs off the field and grabs Franny's hand.

"It's okay," she says. "It's okay."

"No!" he shrieks.

Mr. Darko is steaming. Walt moves fast. He points to Mr. Darko's whistle. "This would be a good time to blow it. Loud."

Mr. Darko blows it loud and long. A couple of dogs start yelping. Benny hollers "No!" like his ears are bursting.

The crowd quiets down a little.

Franny takes Benny back to the bus.

Walt stands on the field, all six foot one inch, 237 pounds, and hollers, "Myerson Middle School! If you continue to boo our team, you will forfeit this game for unsportsmanlike conduct." People get really quiet now. "What," Walt shouts, "would you like to do?"

Danny whispers to me, "Is that a rule?"

"It is now."

The crowd gets quieter.

"What would you like to do?" Walt shouts. "Play for real or boo? You decide."

Their coach runs up. "Listen, guy, sorry 'bout this. People are working through things. Your town hasn't exactly—"

Walt rises up to his full wingspan. "My town, *guy*, is dealing with a bad thing. These boys had nothing to do with that. You either provide visiting teams with a welcoming atmosphere or you forfeit."

The man puts his hands on his hips. "We're not going to forfeit."

Walt takes out his phone. "Fine."

"Who're you calling?"

"The press. They love a nice, juicy story. All kinds of lessons to be learned in this baseball season."

"Whoa, we don't want any bad publicity."

A few more boos are starting. The Myerson coach shouts, "Knock that off!" The people quiet down. He turns to Walt. "We're playing."

"That's what we came to do."

Walt sticks out his hand; the coach shakes it.

"Spit," I tell my guys.

The ground gets wet.

I tell Benchant, "You need to be more irritating than you've ever been. Drive that pitcher up a wall."

"Yeah, Lopper, yeah . . ."

Walt nods to me, walks to the bench, and sits down.

Terrell looks at Walt. "Your dad's cool, Lopper."

Tell me about it.

Have you ever seen an eagle fly? I mean really fly?

Everybody at the Myerson Middle School game did today. Saw him lock his wings and fly higher than the storm.

◆ ◆ ◆

I think this game was more about what happened before the game started than how it ended.

We didn't win according to the scoreboard. But we won every other way.

Benchant stole two bases, and I'm pretty sure by

the end of the game the pitcher had a nervous twitch.

Aiden Oxley bunted and advanced a runner.

Alvin Oxley caught three fly balls in the outfield.

Sky struck out three in a row in the third inning. That Myerson team was getting nervous. I put Donald in left field because everybody needs to play.

"Look scary out there," I told him.

Not one ball headed his way.

And that GO, MUSKRATS! sign was held high for the entire game.

Benny is waiting on the bus for us with Franny. "Yay," he says quietly as we climb on.

Benchant actually smiles. "Thanks, Benny."

Sky says, "You're the best, man."

"Best," Benny whispers.

Chapter
25

I FEEL TIRED, more tired than usual. Like someone turned on a tap and all my energy ran out.

I'm late for school. I needed to sleep longer. When I get there the word is out about the booing.

Mr. Hazard calls the team into his office. He still has the HAZARD sign on his door. Casey, who spends a lot of time in Mr. Hazard's office, shouts, "We're innocent. We have alibis!"

Mr. Hazard's face is red as he paces in front of another sign that says HAZARDOUS CONDITIONS. "I can promise you, boys, what happened yesterday at Myerson is not going to happen again."

"My dad took care of it," I tell him.

"He kicked it," Sky agrees.

"And we're grateful for that." He pauses in front of HAZARDOUS MATERIALS—HAZARDOUS WASTE (that's on his trash can). "Your father won't be the only one kicking, Jeremiah, I assure you. I've heard from many baseball parents who are not going to let this go."

"My mother was there," Sky says. "She was mad."

"Yes. We're serious about supporting you."

Casey raises his hand. "Can we have cheerleaders?"

I elbow him. "We appreciate your support, Mr. Hazard." I stare at the guys until they all say thank you.

"We'd like to honor you in the next assembly," he says.

Alvin raises his hand. "We haven't won yet."

"Not yet." Mr. Hazard smiles. "There will be more to come on this, boys."

Casey asks, "Can we have a parade through town?"

Mr. Hazard sighs.

I say, "Thank you, sir. We're totally grateful. Any games you can get us, I promise you, we'll play like maniacs."

"Yes!" Casey shouts. "We are total—"

Terrell and I push Casey out the door.

◆ ◆ ◆

I'm in English class. The kid behind me is coughing. Not just randomly coughing—he's aiming it at me. I look at him; he coughs deep, doesn't cover his mouth. Covering your mouth is the number one rule of being a responsible cougher.

I can't get sick!

I have low immunity because of my transplant and the medication I have to take. That means I can get sicker than regular people.

And I usually do!

The girl across from me is sneezing. A pile of used tissues are on her desk, like she's proud of the collection.

You should put those away. They're crawling with germs.

"I want you to think creatively," Mrs. Ogletree is saying. "Because writing a poem captures special moments in life. Be expressive! Let your thoughts flow."

We're supposed to write a poem now. Aunt Charity had me do a lot of this.

I let my thoughts flow . . .

I'm surrounded.
Every virus known to man is in this room
Landing on me.
It's like an invasion.

Germ armies marching
Wearing matching helmets
Carrying weapons
Shouting a germ war cry.
I drink chicken soup for lunch because of the
　electrolytes.
I wash my hands dozens of times.
I squirt antiseptic lotion onto my hands and rub
　it on my neck.

"Time's up," Mrs. Ogletree announces. "Anyone want to read their poem?"

I'm not done with mine. I keep writing:

I'm sneezing now
And coughing.
I fought the good fight, but I lost.

I write "The Cold" at the top of my paper and decide not to read it, even though it's good.

◆ ◆ ◆

I don't feel well. I go home right after school, tell Terrell to run practice.

I go to sleep at eight at night—I'm not kidding. And I get sick anyway. Really sick.

Sinus infection, headache, dripping nose, bad cough.

"I'm sorry, Walt."

"You have nothing to apologize for."

He looks so worried, because the last time I got like this, I got bronchitis, which took weeks and weeks to leave my body.

I'm cold, too, and wearing two sweaters plus heavy pants.

I can't go to school. I can't help the baseball team. I have a pillow on the couch and an electric blanket. I'm reading my coaching books, listening to the game, shouting at the game.

I point to the TV. "You've had the bases loaded twice and you can't make it happen? I mean, you're making trillions of dollars. How hard can this be?"

Walt is working at home. He puts SARB on the living room rug. "Find Jeremiah, SARB."

I raise a weak hand; SARB rolls to me, but I have a coughing fit, and I choke from my own coughing, which is so pathetic. SARB can't cope with this and rolls back to Walt.

Walt adds this to his list of things to fix for SARB.

There is no known list of things to fix for me.

I take two pills. I just wanted to come to Hillcrest and be regular—go to baseball games, have a friend. You know, normal.

I look at Walt, who hasn't had a normal day, probably, since he adopted me. And I wonder: was I too much trouble for my mother?

Is that why she . . .

I shake that thought from my mind. There are things we all think about that are guaranteed to make us miserable, and this is one of the big miserables for me.

I attempt laughing, have another coughing fit, and half choke.

I look out the front window. I want to be out there living strong.

I remember those two years when I couldn't do much. I'd look out the window and picture the life I wanted to have. It always involved running and baseball.

Well, I've got the baseball part now—sort of.

Franny and El Grande are by their garage, fixing the rocking horse Bo wanted to throw out. El Grande is tightening the springs with a tool as Franny holds the horse in place. Then El Grande runs his hand over the horse and begins to use sandpaper on it. Franny is smiling and sanding, too. She must have had this rocking horse when she was a kid.

It's good they're restoring it.

A few years ago, Baby lost her left eye when she was attacked by Gerald Cosmo's parakeet, Twinkles. I was so upset, I cried. But Walt got a new eye that almost matched the other one and sewed it onto Baby.

"There," he said. "Better than before."

When I woke up from my surgery, and a million doctors and nurses asked how I was, I told them:

Better than before.

Chapter 26

I WAS IN the hospital for two days and had to miss school. Dr. Dugan's team made a big deal about watching me because I have a sinus infection and they wanted to make sure it didn't turn into something else, like pneumonia. I mentioned there are staph infections that people can only get in hospitals and they should let me go home before things get worse.

I'm home now. I have even more pills to take—you should see my collection—laid out across the kitchen counter in groups based on when I need to take them. My phone is dinging reminders; Jerwal is beeping backup reminders.

And Aunt Charity calls, in case I forget.

"My goal next year is to develop superhuman strength, Walt."

"It's good to have goals. For now, let's take your temperature."

I stick the thermometer in my ear. More beeping. "It's a hundred point eight, Walt. That's hardly anything."

"It indicates infection."

"It's all my energy having no place to go!"

He brings bowls of soup to the table. Benny's mom brought it over. "She made biscuits for us."

I sit down. She's so nice. I reach for a biscuit. These are good.

I've got baseball on the TV and radio day and night. St. Louis had the bases loaded three times and couldn't score a run.

"When you look in the mirror tomorrow morning," I say to the Cardinals on TV, "what do you want to see?"

CORRECT ANSWER: *A winner, Coach!*

Terrell calls and says that practice is going okay.

"Okay" is not acceptable.

"Mr. Darko is doing drills with us, but they're more like soccer drills. We're mostly running."

"What about hitting and throwing and catching?"

"He's not into that as much."

This is unbelievable!

Lopper, there comes a time when you must summon the strength within you and press forward to your ultimate goal.

I feel a little weak, so I sit down. Actually, lying down is better.

I cover myself with another blanket and watch SARB try to go through the maze I built with my baseball books. SARB stops at *The Science of Hitting* by Ted Williams.

I tell him, "It's a little slow at first, but then you can't put it down."

SARB backs into *The Boys of Summer* and gives up.

"He might not like the classics, Walt."

◆ ◆ ◆

My fever broke last night. I am wrapped in a blanket when Franny comes over.

"This looks like a blanket," I tell her, "but it's actually giving me a powerful electrical charge that will transform me into—"

"You look pale."

"I'm still charging."

I let her in. Then I realize this place looks like a hospital room! My pills are on the table, the humidifier is pumping steam into the room, and Baby is on a chair in her bag.

"Wow," she says. "You were sick."

I try to pick things up—take all my pill bottles off the table along with the supersize Lysol spray disinfectant.

"You should see our house when I get sick, Jeremiah. I have four teddy bears out, and they're not as good as . . ." She looks at Baby. "What is that?"

"An eagle."

She smiles. "Benny drew this for you." She hands me a painting of balloons and squiggles:

She points to the top. "It's a bird."

"That's nice."

It looks like a canary—small and yellow. But it's flying. Of course, there's a big difference between flying and soaring. Soaring happens when you don't have to flap your wings—you're carried by the wind.

"Can I use your bathroom?"

I point down the hall. Franny heads there. I throw a towel over my pill collection.

I hear, "Uh, Jeremiah . . ." I look and see Franny standing in front of the bathroom door, confused.

"That's the door," I tell her. She doesn't move. Then I remember the NO ROBOTS IN THE BATHROOM BY ORDER OF THE MANAGEMENT sign.

"You're not a robot, Franny; you can go in."

Jerwal stands by the door to greet her when she comes out.

Not everyone could live in this house.

Chapter

27

I'M NOT LISTENING to the news anymore. Nobody is getting it. Baseball, they say, is dead here.

Hello!

We're playing baseball here.

We have bats and gloves and everything!

It's Monday morning, I'm in school, and we now have thirteen players. I'm not kidding! Terrell recruited another pitcher, Jupiter Jetts.

"He can't pitch long like Sky," Terrell says. "He's a closer."

That means he pitches the last few innings and makes sure we win. Middle school teams don't usually have a closer, but we're here to change that. Middle school teams don't usually have trouble finding other teams to play them, either.

But it's always something. By Monday afternoon,

we're down to twelve players again. Casey Bean, our relief pitcher, quits. His brother, Rick, was a Hornet.

"My dad says I have to run track, Jeremiah."

"But we need you."

Casey shakes his head sadly. "It's not happening. I'm sorry. All the stuff got to be too much . . ."

Benchant walks up. "You're not quitting," I tell him.

"My dad's giving me a hard time about baseball, Lopper."

"You can't quit, Benchant. We'll work it out."

I find Mr. Hazard in the cafeteria.

"Sir, we have a problem, and I know you'll want to help."

"What's going on, Jeremiah?"

"The baseball team is shrinking, sir. We're down to twelve players and we might lose Benchant. Parents want their kids to play another sport because of the Hornets."

Mr. Hazard paces in front of the salad bar. I don't mention it's crawling with bacteria and if he gets too close—zap!

I let him pace a little longer. Vice principals usually need extra pacing time. "I was wondering if you could talk to the parents and encourage them, as you are so good at doing, sir. Inspire them about the power of baseball and how this middle school team is important. Not quitting is a great lesson for us all to learn right now."

Mr. Hazard stops. "How old are you again?"

"Probably twelve. Possibly older."

He gives me a strange look, which I'm used to. "I'll call the parents. I'll see what I can do. Do you want me to talk to the team?"

"At some point, yes. That would be great."

"We're going to get this team the help you need. That's a promise. I wasn't sure about baseball fitting in here, to be honest, but now . . ."

"Baseball fits everywhere, Mr. Hazard."

His eyes get that Baseball Is Life look. "You know, I was a catcher in high school." He crouches down by the napkin dispenser like a catcher. This is a big moment for him. It takes him a while to stand back up, but it was a great effort. "We want to keep this team together, Jeremiah. We want to support our—"

"Muskrats."

"I wonder who picked that name."

"It's unclear."

◆ ◆ ◆

It didn't help that we had our worst game yet against the Brownsville Badgers, who ruled the seven long innings, twelve to nada. Danny kept asking, "Can we go home yet?"

And the Badgers had these smirks on their faces like we were jokes.

It was Jupiter's first game, too. He kept throwing junk. Roy Nader missed umpteen catches. I've never been happier when a game was over.

We are quiet on the bus, except for a few groans. Misery does this. But as the bus rolls past the Hornets' Nest, we see a crowd . . . then we see why.

CHEATERS

It's written in black spray paint across the front of the stadium.

A TV crew is filming. Our bus driver actually stops! A reporter faces the camera. "The investigation into the role of steroid use at Hillcrest High is now going back six years. Will six years of championship wins be in jeopardy? What will it mean for this little town once fueled by baseball glory?"

I lower my head. It will mean more parents want their kids off our team.

But Franny says, "It means that people better start supporting the middle school team, because you're as clean as it gets."

"Yay!" Benny shouts.

The three of us walk home from school not saying anything. When we turn onto Weldon Road, Bo is lugging a trunk out from the garage. Franny gasps and backs up. Benny sees his dad and runs over shouting, "We lost, Daddy! We lost!"

"That's okay." Mr. Lewis gives him a big hug. "Everybody loses sometimes."

Adler trots over to say hello. I pat him. "Good dog."

But the trunk . . .

"I . . ." Bo begins. "I didn't know it was in there. It had a tarp over it."

Franny looks at the dusty trunk. It has stickers on it from Chicago, Kansas City—the others are ripped and faded. *Play Ball!* is painted across it.

Mrs. Engers walks out of the garage like she's holding herself together. "I thought he'd lost it."

Franny bites her lip. "Guess not."

"It's locked," Bo adds quietly. The lock is rusted.

Franny looks at me sadly. "It's our dad's trunk, Jeremiah."

Oh.

They stare at it, and I remind myself—four years ago, something happened to this family.

"Do you want to open it?" Bo asks her.

"No." Franny and her mom say this together.

Bo stands there at first, and then carries the trunk back to the garage.

Chapter 28

THE *HILLCREST HERALD* comes out with an editorial that goes viral—in Hillcrest, at least.

El Grande reads it to Franny and Bo. Mrs. Prim gets on the phone and reads it to her granddaughter. Walt and I take turns reading it. It's one of those times when a good voice breaks out and helps just about everybody.

Walt leans against the refrigerator to help his back and begins: "'What Really Happened in Hillcrest? by Mark T. Inslow. For as long as I can remember, Hillcrest has been a baseball town. Winning. Losing. Winning. Losing . . . and then Coach Perkins came. And we stopped losing. We *won*. Big games. Big championships. After a while, you forget about losing. Being the best year after year means you'd better stay there. Nothing short of it is acceptable.

"'I wonder if I should have been asking more questions. I'd come to expect nothing short of winning from this team of champions. The truth is, the team—and many in our town—became addicted to winning. It was good for the boys, for the town, for the school, for . . . You fill in the blank.

"'Now we know it was too good to be true. Hargie Cantwell's fastball is forever a memory, and baseball in Hillcrest, so big and bold, made us the worst kind of famous.'"

Walt sighs deeply and hands the paper to me. I sit at the table and read the next part.

"'What do we tell the kids? Here's what I'm telling mine: It's okay to lose; it's okay to not be number one year after year. Taking steroids in sports is cheating. And cheating, even if almost everybody else is doing it, is wrong. Winning by cheating isn't winning. It's losing. And losing by honorable efforts can be the biggest win of your life.

"'I hope we won't just toss our Hornets hats in a growing pile by the stadium and shake our angry fists at being tricked. We don't need anger as much as we need courage. Courage is at its best when there isn't much of it around. So if you feel the stirrings of that, please step out and help us rebuild. Let's give the media something else to talk about.'"

I stand here holding the paper. "I swear, Walt, if there was a place to enlist, I'd go and do it."

"Jer, I think you already have."

◆ ◆ ◆

I draw a beard on the mother on the front of the cheesiest Mother's Day card I can find. I paste a picture of a laptop in the mother's hand. Inside it says:

> *Mother dear,*
> *How can I thank you*
> *for every year*
> *and every tear?*

I put an X through that and write:

Walt, You rock!

I hand it to Walt. I always get my dad a Mother's Day card, and he always groans, like now.

"This might be the worst yet, Jer."

I smile. "Thanks."

"Where do you find these things?"

Cards this bad don't fall from the sky. "I had to look hard, Walt. I got it at the Peaceful Lutheran second-hand store."

Walt dips an extreme Nutella cookie into his coffee. "You made these?"

"Benny's mom's recipe."

"This cookie requires full concentration, Jer." He eats it slowly, sips the coffee. "You've outdone yourself."

We're eating hamburgers on our back porch. Regular people tend to have cookies after their hamburgers, but our number one Mother's Day rule is Dessert Comes Whenever You Want It.

Walt has another cookie. "Listen, to change the subject for a minute: I've got a dinner tomorrow night."

"Okay."

Cough. "It's, uh, not a business thing."

"Okay."

"It's a dinner with a . . . person."

"Eating with a person is good, Walt, as opposed to, say, eating with a buffalo."

"A female person, Jer."

Oh.

He coughs. "A female person who is also a doctor."

"What kind of a doctor?"

Another cough. "A cardiologist."

"Would that be my cardiologist?"

He nods.

"My personal cardiologist?"

He nods.

"How did this happen?"

"I called her when you were sick because I was worried, and we got to talking. I wasn't planning to bring up dinner, but it kind of spilled out." He looks happy. "You're cool with this?"

"You haven't been on a date, Walt, since—"

"This isn't a date. It's dinner."

I was about to say Margie in Toronto, who I didn't like at all, as opposed to Dr. Dugan, who I like a lot.

"It's not a date," Walt repeats.

Whatever you say, Walt. "Where are you going?"

"There's a new fish place I heard about." He smiles. "Cardiologists like fish. It's good for the heart."

I'm smiling, too.

"What?" he says.

"Nothing."

"I'm finding this irritating, Jer."

I'm smiling big as we head to the front lawn to play catch.

◆ ◆ ◆

Something called a preliminary hearing is taking place tomorrow to look at the evidence piling up against Coach Perkins. That's the next step in the process. After that, Walt told me, the case goes to a grand jury. All of this has to happen before there can be an official trial. Coach Perkins is saying through his lawyers that he's not guilty—the truth will come out.

Lying and steroids seem to go together like peanut butter and jelly. Most of the athletes I've heard about who were accused of using PEDs lie at first. They're very good at this. Then later they admit they lied and apologize. I don't ever want to be a good liar. It would make it too easy to keep doing it.

I look out my bedroom window. So many stars are out tonight. My favorite star fact is: stars die but can keep on glowing. I like stubbornness in a star.

A couple of streetlights are on. Two more hours and Mother's Day is over. I've tried to picture what my mother was like—was she tall or short or skinny or always on a diet? Did she have a big laugh or a quiet one? Did she like baseball? I just want to know one thing about her.

I've asked Walt, "You don't remember some desperate-looking mother around the office? She could have come in at night and cleaned the building. She was probably watching you."

"Believe me, Jer, I've tried to remember any little thing, but . . ."

"She was probably shy, Walt. She might not have spoken very good English."

Walt would hold up both hands and shake his head.

Uncle Jack always told me, "When you don't know something, focus on all the stuff you do know."

I get a piece of paper and write:

Hey, Mom.

Baby and I are fine, although he needs a plastic bag to stay together. So far, I don't.

Happy MD, wherever you are. You were right about Walt.

J

Chapter 29

AT SCHOOL I have three pop quizzes. Then a substitute teacher in science says we can't make compounds in class until Ms. Mullner gets back. Danny raises his hand and says Ms. Mullner said we could make gunpowder—a world-famous compound. This is so not true. Franny shoots him a look.

The substitute smiles. "No gunpowder on my shift."

"I just want to hear the noise—that's all!"

Then it rains, which means no baseball.

The school bus drives past the Hornets' Nest. They did a good job of cleaning off the CHEATERS word, but some words just stay in places long after you can't hear or see them anymore.

When I get home, Donald Mole is sitting on my porch. "Can I talk to you?" he asks.

I'm tired, but I sit down. "Will you help me get

better, Jeremiah? I'll really work hard. I know I'm not great at baseball, but I love it. I want to be better."

I wish we could play catch right now, but it's raining too hard.

He looks at his glove. "I know what you're thinking. I can't run, hit, or throw . . ."

"I wasn't thinking that. I was thinking, what are you best at?"

He studies his glove. "I'm best at figuring things out."

I stand up. "That's a great thing, Donald. People like you can make things happen."

"Yeah?" He stands, too.

I'm processing this . . .

"Okay, Donald, remember the last practice? You weren't catching the ball well. What was happening?"

He's processing. "After I missed a couple, I got embarrassed and I stopped trying."

"I know exactly what that's like."

"You do?"

"And do you know what you can do? You approach this in a new way. Let's figure it out. The ball"—I hold up my baseball—"is coming toward you, Donald."

"Is it in the air or on the ground?"

"The air."

He looks up a little. "Okay."

"Show me how you catch it."

He holds up his glove and pinches it together.

"Donald, you have to have your glove open to catch the ball. If you get a piece of it, you close your glove tight around it like a clam. Practice that—opening and closing. And then the ball is coming toward you nice and easy, your glove is open . . ."

Donald is looking up, his arm is up . . .

"And you say to yourself, 'I've got this. I've got this.'"

"I've got this," he whispers. "I've got this."

"Practice that."

"I will."

"Can I see your glove?" He hands it to me. It's new and stiff. I tell him about breaking in the leather and making the glove part of his hand. "Mess it up."

He starts doing that. The rain is down to a sprinkle. "Come on." I get my glove.

I throw underhand to him. He catches a few, and when he does, his face glows.

He throws it back to me, I reach to catch it, throw it back.

"That's it, Donald. That's it."

He catches three in a row and starts laughing. "You

know what, Jeremiah? Two years ago, I had cancer. And my big wish was to play baseball." He throws the ball back to me. It lands in the bushes, but that's okay. I get the ball. I'll tell him about my hospital stuff another time.

"Donald, it's happening. You're doing it!"

◆ ◆ ◆

I tell Walt about this as he changes shirts five times before he settles on the first one—blue—for his this-is-not-a-date dinner with Dr. Dugan.

"Don't say it." He heads for the door.

I walk him to the car. I feel like I should give him some tips—like, Don't drop your phone. Don't drop your fork. "Good luck, Walt."

"Thanks, Jer."

He pulls out of the driveway. I wave good-bye.

I just hope this doesn't mess things up for me, because Dr. Dugan seems like a very good cardiologist.

I go back inside and watch the eagle cam for inspiration. The eggs are still eggs—no baby eagle beaks pecking through. The father eagle is sitting on the nest.

You go, man!

But the dad starts moving. What's going on? He moves off one of the eggs, and I see it. A little crack. This is major! *Come on, baby.* Now the eagle dad is acting upset. Another viewer says there are two other eagles flying overhead.

The mother flies back to the nest. The father screeches. It's good they're together right now. I think this would be much harder for a single parent to do, although not impossible.

And now the cam stops working! Oh, come on! This happens sometimes, but not now. I wait, but get nothing.

I suppose I should have dinner, but I'm not really hungry. I'll just close my eyes for a minute, then do my homework . . .

◆ ◆ ◆

"You're still up?"

I look around. Walt is standing here. "I think I fell asleep."

"Homework was that fascinating?"

I shake my head clear. "How did it go, Walt?"

He scratches his beard. "The restaurant was good."

"Good."

"I had sautéed grouper with pistachios; Sarah had salmon with pineapple chutney."

"Good."

"I'm going to bed." He touches my shoulder. "You should, too."

I fold my arms across my chest. "Did the dinner turn into a date?"

Walt freezes. Doesn't turn around. "As a matter of fact, Jer, yes. It did." He heads to his room. "Lights out in five."

I see the clock. Twelve seventeen. That's twelve as in midnight.

I've got questions.

Is my life going to change, Walt?

And how much longer do we have here? What are they telling you at work? Does this at least mean you need to get your contract renewed? Because I'd start working on that now if I were you.

We need to stay in Hillcrest as long as we can. Right?

I need to find out what happened with Franny's dad. The team has to win at least once before I go. And if I wasn't so tired, I'd think of more stuff that will keep us here.

Sorry, Yaff. Really, really sorry.

Chapter 30

THEY DIDN'T ALLOW TV cameras in the courtroom
during Coach Perkins's preliminary hearing, but the
Hillcrest Herald published parts of the transcript
(the actual wording of what people said). None of
the names of the Hornets players were used because
they are under eighteen.

Did Coach Perkins give you pills?
—Yes.

What did he say they were for?
—He said they were vitamins.

**Did you receive injections from Coach Per-
kins?**
—Yes. I mean, he didn't give them. A lady
came and gave the shots.

Who was this woman?
—*I don't know.*

Why did you consent to this?
Objection, Your Honor.
Objection overruled. Answer the question,
please.
—*He said they would help our muscles bounce*
back from injury. I just figured he knew. I
trusted him. He was my coach.

Did you feel different after the injections?
Objection, Your Honor . . .

Did Coach Perkins tell you what you might
experience after the injections?
—*He said we would feel more pumped, but that*
meant it was working.

Did you experience side effects?
—*My mom said I talked back more . . . I got*
zits on my back.

Another player said:

—*We should have known. We should have*
thought about it.

Mrs. Rooney said:

—*I missed some clues along the way. I'm
ashamed to say that, but I did.*

Coach Perkins said:

—*I love these boys like they are my own.
I'm saddened by this—I can't tell you how
it grieves me. But the pills I gave them
were vitamins. I don't know what they got
into on their own, but they didn't get steroids from me.*

That got people screaming in town.

It's good to know these things, but Walt said not to focus on it. "Jer, you've got higher business to take care of."

◆ ◆ ◆

Right before English class, Mrs. Ogletree waves me to her desk.

"Jeremiah, I think you're a good and concise writ-er, but I'm concerned that you're only writing about baseball. I would like to see you branch out . . ."

"I wish I could," I tell her. "But I need to stay focused right now." I hand her my sentences that show hyperbole, which is a fancy word for exaggeration. I worked hard on these.

- The weight of the world was on the coach's shoulders as he looked at the scoreboard and knew his dream of winning the World Series was only a mirage.
- When he pitched, the screaming eagle swooped over the plate, coming in for the kill.
- The outfielder was so hungry, he could eat a horse.

She looks at my paper and back at me. "We'll need to talk about this again, Jeremiah."

"After the season is over, ma'am."

I take my seat behind Franny, who whispers, "Our game with the Vipers got canceled."

"Why?"

She shrugs.

Logo leans in. "They decided not to play us."

Just great! I expected more from vipers than this.

We need to do something before we rust.

I forgot it's a half school day because the teachers have an afternoon meeting. That means no practice after school.

But as my bus pulls out, I see Donald Mole on the field throwing to Terrell. Again and again. And he's getting it. I wish these bus windows opened! I shout, "Yes! That's the way!" The kids on the bus look at me like I'm strange.

I am strange! "Baseball is back from the dead!" I shout.

I'm not sure if this is hyperbole or just plain fact, but not one person cheers.

◆ ◆ ◆

"You want to walk with me, Jeremiah?" Bo asks. "Not far. A couple blocks."

"Okay." I figure he might want to talk. "How are you doing?"

He shrugs, looks at the envelope he's holding. We turn right on Old Church Road and walk to Fullerton. At Spaulding, Bo turns left.

I know where we're going.

Bo walks toward Hargie's house. It's painted white.

All the shutters are closed. The flowers in the garden are dying. It feels like sadness has crept over everything on this block. We stand here. Then Bo puts the envelope in the mailbox.

"I wrote something to his parents. You know."

"That's nice," I say.

Bo shrugs again. He puts his hands in his pockets and looks at the house.

"I don't think he knew. I don't think Hargie knew what he was taking."

I just listen.

"Because he loved the game. He lived it."

Bo stands there some more. The sun is shining over the Cantwells' roof, glowing bright and sure.

"I wanted to be on that team," Bo says. "I wanted to be a Hornet bad. Coach Perkins told me, work like a demon on the middle school team. Do more, be better than anybody, never quit. That's how you become a Hornet. When he talked to me, it was like . . . he knew everything. He had this power about him. You wanted to do whatever he said."

Bo picks up a stick and throws it.

"The middle school coach, Bordin, said if we complained, we were babies. The umpires hated him, the other coaches hated him. He got thrown out of games for shouting that they were idiots. I kept my mouth shut, I did the drills, I played hurt. Perkins told me, keep it up. I'd be a Hornet. Hargie said when it happened, it would be the best day of my life. I did summer baseball last year before I started high school. I threw out my pitching arm. I can play catch. That's it. Not enough to . . ." His voice trails off.

"That's hard, man."

"Let's go." We cross the street, head back home down Old Church Road.

"Thanks," he says to me.

I nod. He sits on his porch steps thinking. I stand there wondering.

Is Bo right? Did Hargie not know?

Did his parents not see him changing?

Did the other players get fooled?

Are we being fooled?

The sun is brighter now. I'm picturing it warming the sky over Hargie's house of sadness.

El Grande comes on the porch, smiling. "Craziest thing," he says. He takes off his glasses, cleans them on his shirt. "Dr. Selligman of the middle school called me and asked if I would consider coaching the baseball team."

I freeze.

"And old fool that I am, I said yes."

Bo is grinning. I'd better smile.

"That's great!" I shout.

"And," he continues, "Bo, if you're ever inclined to stop by after school and lend a hand, we could use your wisdom."

I smile big, so big it hurts, so big that no one can see that I feel like a heavy door just got slammed in my face.

"That's great!" I say again.

El Grande's phone rings. This is good—I can leave.

The sky is so blue. A perfect baseball day . . .

I wave and walk across the street.

Head up, Lopper. Shoulders strong.

I go inside my house, close the door, shut my eyes.

No crying.

Ex-coaches don't cry.

Chapter
31

I HAD ALL these plans. Not that I told anybody.

I pictured Walt getting off early once a week and helping me coach. I pictured us winning after a few more games and someone doing an article on me as the youngest coach ever.

The problem with picturing is it's not real, even if you put a frame around it.

I sit in our kitchen feeling like I just got fired. That's stupid, I know, seeing as I was never hired . . .

"Jerwal, wake up."

A glow, a beep. He's waiting for my next command. I don't have one.

This was supposed to be a fun place. I left my science fair project and Yaff for baseball and robots. Most of the robots are still falling over. Baseball doesn't need me.

"I'm not their coach, Jerwal." He rolls over and

stops near me. "But I loved being out there. I felt like I was really part of a baseball team." He lifts his arm and glows.

A knock at the front door.

I don't feel like getting up, but I do.

"Come on, Jerwal."

Jerwal and I head down the hall.

El Grande is at the door.

I open it.

"Hello, Jeremiah." He looks strangely at my robot. "And you again."

Jerwal makes a robot noise. El Grande coughs. This might be more than he can handle.

"Jerwal, go to sleep." The robot shuts down.

"We've got business to discuss," El Grande explains. "You left before I could tell you. Here's what I told that principal." He points at me. "I said if I took that coaching job, I'd want you to help. Full-time."

What?

"I'm a good coach, and I've always worked my tail off. But if you think I'm going to stand in front of fifteen middle school baseball players every day—"

"The team is shrinking, sir. We're down to twelve . . . maybe eleven."

"Well, even more proof I need a serious right-hand man to keep me on track."

"That's me?"

"That's you, son. You decide if that works for you. Talk to your father. I'll talk to him, if you want."

"Wow. I would love to do this." But I can't not tell him about Walt's contract. "Full disclosure, El Grande: I'm hoping we'll be here through June, but I don't know."

"Hate to see you go, but I'm willing to take whatever we can get of your time. You're a valuable asset."

I am?

We shake hands. I try to act like I do this all the time, but who am I kidding?

I grin. "What do you want me to do, Coach?"

He folds his arms across his chest. "Whatever I tell you."

◆ ◆ ◆

El Grande gets out of his car and walks slowly to the baseball diamond.

It's like a movie western when the sheriff comes to town to clean up whatever.

The wind blows across the field. El Grande nods at

me, and I feel his power. He takes his glasses off, cleans them on his shirt, puts them back on, and squints. Squinting is a big part of baseball management.

The guys look at him.

"You've got a game," he says.

They chew and spit.

He nods. "What are you guys best at?"

"Losing," Logo says. Terrell pushes him; the others laugh nervously.

Arms crossed tight. "Is that right? I'm standing here with a bunch of losers?"

They look at me. El Grande does, too. "Is that right, Jeremiah?"

"No, I don't think so. I think we've lost some games—three, actually—but that doesn't make us losers."

El Grande walks back and forth. His right leg has a little hobble in it. "What makes a loser?"

They look down.

"Jeremiah?"

"Uh . . ." I take out my phone. Technically, I'm not in school, I'm on the field, so the phone rules don't apply. I go to my thesaurus. Loser . . . loser . . . This is bad.

El Grande points to me. I cough. "Well, a loser isn't

just someone who gets defeated. A loser is a failure, an underachiever, a write-off, has-been, misfit, freak, unpopular person, flop, washout."

El Grande asks the guys, "Are you losers?"

Terrell steps forward. "No, sir."

The rest of the boys step forward and say no and drag Logo with them.

"So let's redefine this. You started late in the season. You've lost a grand total of three games in a row."

Handro raises his hand. "We got booed once."

El Grande pushes his glasses down his nose. "Looks like you survived." He's walking again. "Need I remind you of the great turnarounds in baseball history? The New York Yankees won the pennant after losing seven straight games. The Atlanta Braves rose to the World Series after crushing losses. The Cincinnati Reds couldn't even find their locker room for the first month of the 2012 season, but they came back hard and fast to make the playoffs. How did they do that?"

The team looks to me.

"Jeremiah?" El Grande barks.

"Uh . . . well . . . They got down to . . . I'm making a guess here . . . the fundamentals of the game."

El Grande nods. "That is absolutely right."

Whew.

Hands on his hips. "Fundamentals, gentlemen. Getting on base. Baseball is about getting on base."

The guys spit, which I think is appropriate. Donald misses the ground and spits on his shoe.

"You've got some attitude going here. I like that. We don't have time to practice—we've got a game. But I'm going to tell you what winners don't do. They don't look down or slump their shoulders."

The team is standing up, squaring their shoulders, chewing big.

"I'm giving you one tip. It's for everybody, no matter what position you play. Keep your eye on the ball. You're . . . What's the name of this team?"

I swallow hard. "The Muskrats."

El Grande looks at me. "Where did that come from?"

"No one knows, sir."

El Grande again: "I mean, a muskrat is . . ."

I take out my phone, look it up. It's not good. "A large semiaquatic North American rodent with a musky smell, valued for its fur."

The team looks at one another.

"Benchant smells pretty bad," Danny mentions.

"Shut up, Lopez."

El Grande looks at them. "Is *Muskrat* on your uniforms?"

"No, sir! They just say Hillcrest Middle School."

"We can be grateful for the little things."

Alvin says, "There's a Muskrat banner in the gym."

"But it's ripped," Alex says.

"Rodents rip stuff," their brother Aiden adds.

"Are you three together?" El Grande asks them.

"They're the Oxley brothers," I explain. "Our outfield."

El Grande nods. "We've got oxen in the outfield."

Everybody laughs. He looks at the team. "Have you thought of another name for the team?"

I smile. It all becomes clear to me. "I was thinking, sir, we could be the Eagles."

This rips through the air like a strong wind.

El Grande: "I like that, Jeremiah. I like that very much. An eagle heart. Good eyesight. Fierce."

"Hey." Danny sticks out his hands like they're wings. "I'm a flying muskrat."

"You're our third baseman, son?"

Danny nods.

El Grande thinks about that in a way that should

make Danny nervous. "I'll be having meetings with your parents. We want them to know what we're about. We want them to be part of this effort. Now let's get to that game."

We climb in the bus. Mr. Hazard is sitting in the back. "You're looking strong, guys. Looking tough."

"We got a name transplant!" Danny shouts.

No. A transplant is a lot more complicated. I pass out gum. The team looks at one another, chews, and nods. Nobody slumps.

Franny and Benny climb on the bus. Franny's wearing her glove.

"It doesn't mean anything, Jeremiah."

"We're eagles now," I tell her.

"You always were eagles." She says it loud so everyone can hear.

Chapter

32

IT'S INTERESTING WHAT happens when people get encouraged. Walt taught me that when someone decides not to give up on you, it's proof positive that you'd better not give up on yourself.

There wasn't enough gum or encouragement in the world to help the Eagles win, but I will say we looked tough losing, and we didn't lose by much: 3–2. If Logo hadn't dropped the ball at home plate when a Thunderbolt runner raced in to score, if Benchant hadn't bobbled the ball when Greenville's first baseman bunted and brought the kid on third base home, if the umpire wasn't half blind, we might have won.

But two big things happened.

Our fan base is growing. We had six parents cheering for us, but no one shouted as loudly as Mr. Hazard, who, as a vice principal, has a big voice and isn't afraid to use it.

The other thing was, the loss didn't seem like the others. It almost seemed like a win.

Back on the bus, El Grande says, "I saw some nice plays. Sky, you were throwing to Logo's glove and finding that strike zone. Alvin, you caught two high flies on the run."

Alvin smiles. "My goal was to catch one."

El Grande nods. "Anyone else have a goal for this game?"

Danny says, "I'm not trying to be a moron, but—"

"You don't have to try, Danny," someone says.

"Let him talk. Go on, son."

"I didn't want to leave the field embarrassed."

"I had that goal any number of times when I was playing. And did you?"

"No, sir. I wasn't embarrassed."

Mr. Hazard claps. "I like that!"

"We're going to start looking at personal bests we want to achieve in each game. Jeremiah's going to help you figure out what to work on."

Absolutely!

Franny and Benny are in the bus riding back to the

school with us. Benny is looking out the window, waving to people.

El Grande says, "How's that arm, Sky?"

"A little sore."

"How much did you warm up? How many throws before the game?"

"Uh . . ." Sky isn't sure.

"One seven," Benny says.

Seventeen. El Grande and I look at each other.

Benny waves at a car.

El Grande looks back at Benny. "Were you counting pitches, Benny?"

Benny doesn't answer.

Franny says, "Benny, how many pitches did Sky throw today?"

"Six three."

I keep track of these things during a game. I check my phone. It wasn't sixty-three. It was forty-six. But wait a minute. Forty-six during the actual game plus seventeen in warm-up. That's sixty-three!

I show El Grande.

"Benny," El Grande says, "are you writing the numbers down?"

Benny doesn't answer. He looks out the window.

"Sky pitched six seven pitches before that."

"At the Badgers game, Benny?"

He doesn't answer.

I go through my numbers on that game. Sixty-seven pitches. He's right. Why didn't he get the practice ones?

"Was that the game we came late to, Benny?" Franny asks.

"Six seven," he says, bouncing in his seat.

El Grande says, "Did you keep score with a pencil and paper?"

Benny looks confused. He points to his head. "I see."

"You see it?" Mr. Hazard sits by them. "Benny, how many people are there on this bus?"

Benny doesn't look to check. "One eight," he says instantly.

I count. It's seventeen, actually. Twelve Eagles, me, El Grande, Franny, Benny, and Mr. Hazard. You can't bat a thousand.

But wait a minute. I forgot the bus driver.

That's eighteen!

Mr. Hazard says, "Benny, what do you see on the street?" He points out the window.

"Two one, five, six, five seven."

I don't know what he is counting, but I doubt he's wrong.

The bus pulls into the school parking lot. We get off. Kids are telling Benny, "Way to go."

"You've got a gift, son," El Grande tells him. "One whale of a gift."

◆ ◆ ◆

That night I make the cards.

BASEBALL IS BACK AT HILLCREST MIDDLE SCHOOL

Below that is a picture of a soaring eagle. In the lower right corner it reads:

> The Eagle has landed.
> Come watch us play ball.

We need name recognition fast. I print a ton of these cards.

"Pass these out around town," I tell the Eagles. "Let them know we're here. And don't act dumb about it. We want people to love us."

Chapter

33

I SHOW ONE of the cards to Adler, who sniffs it. "Tell the other dogs, Adler. You need to do your part." I'm watching Franny's house—no sign of her yet this morning. "Adler, it's Saturday. I want you to let me know the minute you see Franny, okay? I need to talk to her."

Adler cocks his head and looks at me.

"You could go by her front door like you're injured. You could cry and whine. What do you think?"

Adler doesn't want to do that.

"Okay, so we're waiting here." I take out my phone. "Adler is an unusual name for a dog. Do you know what your name means? My name, Jeremiah, means 'exalted of God,' which is a lot to live with. Let's see. Adler . . ." I'm scrolling through names. Aaron, Abner . . .

You've got to be kidding. I look at this dog. "Adler,

in German your name means 'eagle.' This is deep. Do you understand? You're one of us!"

Adler wags his tail, and now Franny walks out her door, dressed like she's going for a run.

I wave. "Can I talk to you, Franny?"

She jogs over.

"I need to tell you something."

"What?"

Last night Walt told me he thought we'd be here through June seventh, which is not a lot of time. "But," he told me seriously, "I'm hoping that will change."

"Me too, Walt. Is there anything you—"

"It's complicated, Jer. I don't mean to be mysterious."

This is not like my dad, but when you're not sure how many days you have left in a place, you have to decide to not let things stop you.

So I tell her. About the snack room, and Walt finding me, and my mother leaving the baby eagle for me to gnaw on.

"You're kidding." She sits on the grass.

I tell her about the note on my baby chair. My heart transplant. I tell her almost everything, except the fact that I almost died and that my new heart is named Alice.

She sits there looking at me.

"And I don't know, Franny. I've always thought something hard, maybe not like that exactly, might have happened to you."

She sighs deeply and folds her arms tight across her chest. "Something did happen."

I wait for her to tell me and she doesn't. I don't think this is fair.

"I told you close to everything about my life, Franny."

"What did you leave out?"

"Unimportant, random stuff."

"Like what?" She's waiting.

Okay, you asked for it.

"My favorite color: gold. Favorite food: barbecue."

She leans back on her elbows.

"Favorite baseball player: Jackie Robinson. Second favorite: Lou Gehrig. Third favorite: Roberto Clemente. Is this boring you?"

She laughs. "A little!"

"Then tell me what happened to you or I won't stop."

She shakes her head.

"Favorite cereal: Cheerios."

"Cheerios?"

"Everyone loves Cheerios. Favorite small, adorable animal: brown bunny."

"Awww . . ."

"Favorite large, ugly animal: rhinoceros."

"Baby rhinos are cute!"

"Favorite arthropod: centipede. Favorite punctuation mark: semicolon. Favorite scientific fact: stars die but keep shining."

"They do?"

"Favorite cookie: potato chip. You crush a whole bag of chips to make them. Favorite seven-word joke: A duck walks into a bar. Ouch." That always broke Uncle Jack up.

She doesn't laugh.

I'm speeding through. "Favorite superhero: Iron Man. Favorite eagle: golden. Favorite city: Toronto. Favorite pizza: meatball. Favorite flavor: coffee. Favorite life moment: when Walt found me. Favorite word—"

"Baseball," she says.

I shake my head. "Soar."

"Soar?"

"It's what eagles do more than other birds. They wait for the right air current and they ride it higher than the clouds."

She looks at me. "I've never met a boy like you, Jeremiah."

"Good. I try to be memorable." I lean back, exhausted.

"My dad left," she says.

I sit up.

"Four years ago."

"I'm sorry."

Mrs. Prim is on her porch, trying to listen.

"I don't want to talk about it here, Jeremiah."

"Let's walk. Adler, we'll be back. Good dog."

◆　◆　◆

We are walking through the Peaceful Lutheran Church parking lot, which is a very interesting place, beginning with the sign: LORD, MAKE ME AN INSTRUMENT OF YOUR PEACE.

"I've never seen that in a parking lot before, Franny."

"They don't have enough parking spaces on Sunday. People get pretty worked up."

We're about to sit on a bench. It reads: THE WAGES OF SIN IS DEATH.

I'm sure that's true, but I don't want to sit on it.

The bench in front of the fountain has this:

BE STRONG AND VERY COURAGEOUS.

Much better. We sit on that.

And she tells me . . .

"My dad up and left four years ago and never came back. He left a good-bye note saying he was sorry; he couldn't be part of our family anymore. Bo found the note when he came down for breakfast. It was on the kitchen table." She starts to sway a little. "I don't know why he left. I wonder if it was something about me."

"No," I tell her. "It was about him."

"You didn't know him."

"But I know about this."

It's like a faucet turns on. "He left most of the money and the car. He took his clothes." She's looking at the ground, rocking back and forth. "We were in shock. Benny's mom found out and she came over and cooked for us and helped me and Bo with homework. She helped Mom get out of the house. She was amazing . . . I would do anything for her."

That's why you take care of Benny, I bet.

"And I don't know why, Jeremiah, but I don't remember much about my dad. I can't remember his voice or what we were doing around the time he left, or even what he liked to do. I mean, I know he played baseball. He was on a minor league team. He never made it big. El Grande says he went through life being disappointed."

She closes her eyes. "And I don't want to be like that!"

"You're not."

She shakes her head. "Mom got an investigator to try to find him to pay child support. There was some talk he'd been seen in Canada . . ."

Canada. Okay . . . now I get it.

We sit here on the BE STRONG AND VERY COURAGEOUS bench.

"Did you ever get your dad's trunk open? The one Bo found in—"

"Yes. We opened it."

I wait. "What was inside?"

"Baseball stuff." She's rocking again. "And a map of Canada. That might not mean anything."

Or it might. I wish I had a trunk. A clue.

It starts to rain. "You want to be my best friend in this town?" I ask her.

She looks at the fountain. "Yeah. I think I do."

Chapter 34

WE CAN HEAR the thunder pounding outside. It's supposed to rain for three days, soaking the baseball fields. But inside the batting cages, all is dry.

I convinced Franny to come with the team to practice—it wasn't easy. Benny doesn't come because the sound hurts his ears.

"This pitching machine can be your best friend," I tell them, "or it can beat you bloody. Fast, slow, medium." Every one of the Eagles picks slow. "We'll start there. I want you to keep your eye on the ball, and remember, these will keep coming at you."

Four guys are in four cages.

Four guys swing hard and miss most of the pitches.

Danny in cage three falls down, shouting he's getting attacked by baseballs.

Donald, Terrell, Alvin, and Handro are next. And Donald is on this. He's swinging through, not hitting everything, but he's hitting some. There's a big smile on his face.

"Yes!" I shout to him.

He keeps swinging. "I think I figured out what I'm doing wrong." He turns to me and gets attacked by balls.

"Shut off the machine, Donald!"

Franny is standing there. "I want you to do this," I tell her.

Terrell gets hit by a ball and comes out of the cage rubbing his arm. "Good luck, girl."

She goes inside the cage.

"You turn on the—"

"I know what to do." She turns on the machine to "medium" and stands there, knees bent, bat ready. First pitch, she nails it. Second, again. Third, fourth, fifth—this girl doesn't miss. She's focusing in.

Wham.

Some of the guys are gathering around.

Logo says, "She's good for a girl."

Those words hang there.

"I didn't mean that the way it sounded, I swear!"

Franny glares at him. She turns the machine to "fast." Ball after ball.

Wham.

Crack.

Connect.

Hit after hit.

"That's a homer right there!" I shout. "We win!"

The guy who runs the place comes by. "That's better than yesterday, Franny."

I look at her. "You were here yesterday?"

The guy laughs. "She's been here every day for two weeks. She's a serious hitter."

She shrugs. "Okay, so I'd like to be an Eagle."

"You already are one."

The guys cheer.

◆ ◆ ◆

Batting practice.

Not in a cage.

Walt gets off at four o'clock to come and give us some pointers. He shows us what a fastball looks like coming at you. A curve. A junk ball. One that's going in the dirt.

"Get used to what they look like," Walt says, "and

you'll know when to swing and when not to."

Not swinging isn't one of our specialties.

"Here's a curveball," Walt shouts, "that will not be a strike. Don't swing at this. Watch."

Walt throws and Sky the pitcher watches it whiz by in the dirt.

"Patience is one of the biggest lessons a batter has to learn," Walt explains. "Only swing at the good pitches." Donald is listening to this like his life depends on it. "Make the pitcher throw strikes. You stand there and ignore the junk. Come on, Donald. Batter up." Donald gets in place, waiting. Walt gets ready to throw again. "This is going to be high. You don't bother with this. Watch . . ."

Donald stands there and doesn't swing as the junk ball comes in.

"Okay?"

"Yeah, Mr. Lopper. Okay."

◆　◆　◆

Warm-ups. Sidesteps. Crossovers. Skipping. Walking backward.

El Grande has the team doing it all.

He and I practice signals—and these get weird. Ear

tugging, one nose tap, two nose taps, chest pats, left arm up, right arm up, tug your earlobe.

Benny is very good at copying this. He'll stand next to me and tap his nose and raise his hand exactly right. He's loving the walking backward and the running, too.

"Benny," I say, "you're a good runner."

Benny grins and runs away from me when I say it. He's kind of our mascot and ball boy and statistician rolled into one. Benny's dad, Mr. Lewis, sits with him now that Franny is playing.

A few people come to watch us practice. Hargie's dad comes and sits with Mr. Lewis, but doesn't stay long. "I appreciate what you're doing!" he shouts to us.

Rabbi Tova comes with her little daughter, Hannah, who wants to play first base for the Red Sox. She asks Franny for her autograph. Franny signs it, *Girls on First*.

Mr. Hazard has the team walk onto the stage at assembly as the Hillcrest Middle School marching band plays "We Will Rock You" really badly.

We haven't rocked anybody yet.

Or maybe we have.

Mr. Hazard shows up wearing an eagle costume and starts dancing by our bus. He says he's been looking for an eagle costume since we changed our name. "Most of them looked like chickens," he tells us. "And I wasn't going there." He's a very different man when he's in this outfit.

We've got a new name, a mascot, and a rabbi. Now all we have to do is win.

◆　◆　◆

Winning keeps not happening.

We play badly against the Falcons, and eagles should beat falcons with one wing tied behind their backs. Danny injures his throwing arm in that game—he can't play. Franny takes first base, and Benchant replaces Danny on third.

Our pitching falls apart, too.

We almost win against St. Catherine's, but Logo bobbles the ball on a close play at home plate and we lose, 4–3.

Danny comes to practice in a cast. "I can't play, but I can cheer!" He sits with Benny and they yell, "Go Eagles!"

Yeah, that's us now. But something else is happening. El Grande says it: "A few weeks ago, I would have said you weren't good enough to win, but now you are."

There is something about those words that sends a whoosh through the Eagles, like an air current lifting us higher. We are so ready for our next game against the Tornadoes—we played them before, and now we'll get another shot. But we get rained out! Sky screams that he can pitch in the rain.

"Save that energy for the next game," El Grande tells him.

Chapter
35

WALT AND DR. DUGAN are eating a lot of fish together. I go to a couple of those dinners, and I need to warn any kid: do not go on a date with your father.

I mean, the looks on their faces. The arm around the shoulder. The lowered voices.

Can't you guys just talk in regular voices?

Plus they laugh at things too long that are only a little funny. Walt is trimming his beard more, too. There are little beard hairs in the sink every day as opposed to once a month.

And every time I see Dr. Dugan, I feel I should be getting some kind of examination. I can't call her Sarah. I would never call Dr. Feinberg Irving!

Walt is testing a gray SARB on the kitchen floor. It's moving around Jerwal and then Adler really well.

I stagger across the floor like I've been shot. I'm

groaning a little, whispering, "Help. Help." The SARB rolls up to me and completely shuts down.

I know it takes time to get used to me, but come on!

"What happened?" Walt checks his computer, checks the robot. "Why are you choking?" The SARB gives no clues. Walt picks it up. "You know, little guy, I can relate. I've got something I need to do, and I keep shutting down, too."

I don't know what that is.

"I've got to make a phone call, Jer."

Walt makes the call in his room with the door shut. That means he's probably calling Dr. Dugan.

"Something tells me this is deep, Jerwal." Jerwal and the gray SARB follow me. I try to listen at the door.

Walt shouts, "This is private, Jer."

I have a feeling this is going to affect me, too. Back to the kitchen with the robots. At least I've got company.

◆ ◆ ◆

"Why are you choking out there, Alvin?"

"I'm not getting to the ball in time . . ."

"You're there in time," I tell him.

He shrugs.

"Are you telling yourself you can't catch it?"

"I don't know. Maybe . . ."

Last night I was reading about sports psychology. I will need to get a degree in this. "You know what causes people to choke, Alvin?"

"Swallowing a chicken bone?"

He's serious.

"Not that kind of choking; the kind that causes you to not do something you can do."

Alvin shrugs.

I put my hands in my pockets. "We don't have to talk about this." I start walking away.

"Wait, Jeremiah. What's the choking thing about?"

I turn around. Give him what I learned.

"You don't tell yourself anything except 'I'm going to catch this ball that's coming at me and not run into my brother.'"

"I'm going to catch this ball that's coming at me and not run into my brother," Alvin repeats.

"That's it." I walk away, but I hear him say it again.

"I'm going to catch this ball that's coming at me . . ."

I tell Franny to hit some poppers to Alvin, and you know what? He catches three out of four.

"What happened with that last one?" I shout.

He looks embarrassed. "I didn't tell myself I could catch it."

"Talk to yourself out there, Alvin. Be a little crazy."

He smiles. "Okay, Coach."

Twice now!

Twice I've been called Coach!

◆ ◆ ◆

The Eagles are getting a good rep in town—not for winning, but for being the kind of team that people want to cheer for. I think it's because we love the game and we're good losers. We'll take all the support we can get.

The Brownie Bakery gives us free samples and has a GO EAGLES sign in their window. A bus from the Hillcrest Senior Citizens Center comes to watch us practice. These people have opinions.

I don't think he should be swinging that soon. Doesn't it look like he's swinging too soon, Harold?

That girl out there needs to smile more.

They should have better seats. More people would come if there were better seats.

Pay attention, young man. You're dropping too many balls!

Mr. Hazard puts on his eagle costume, puts his

arm around the old ladies, and shakes his wings. Everyone has a good time. That's what we're about. Come cheer for us—we'll do our best to win, and we promise you'll have fun.

But not everyone in town cares about that.

The team is having pizza at Junk Ball to celebrate that we're getting better. Chip Gunther of Chip Gunther's Sports is at a nearby table with his friends. He looks over at us, shakes his head like we're morons, and says loudly so everybody can hear, "When that middle school team stops playing like turkeys, I'll support them."

He laughs so mean. The men who are with him at the table laugh, too.

"Don't let it get to you," I tell the guys.

"Nothing but turkeys," Mr. Gunther repeats.

Donald looks at me. "Your dad said when junk comes at you, don't swing."

I try not to listen to the junk, but Chip Gunther is still laughing, and now he's saying, "Gobble, gobble . . ."

I stand up. Turning an eagle into a turkey? No, sir, I can't handle that.

Swoop.

I stand at Chip Gunther's table. His face is either

red from laughing or too much beer—I can't tell. And I don't care.

"Mr. Gunther, you just called the middle school baseball team turkeys. Is that right, sir?"

He's laughing. "You've got that right, kid."

"Mr. Gunther, you were the head of the committee that brought Coach Perkins to town. I'd say you don't know the difference between a turkey and an eagle."

"Whoa, boy!" says one of the men.

Chip Gunther stands up. "Who do you think you are, kid?"

The Eagles gather around me. "He's our assistant coach," Terrell explains.

"No wonder you can't win." Chip Gunther is laughing big, but nobody is laughing with him.

I stare at him. "I'm asking you to never use that word to describe our team, Mr. Gunther. We've worked hard to get better, and we're going to keep it up. We want to win, but we're not going to cheat to do it. We're not turkeys, Mr. Gunther. We're eagles."

Some people in the restaurant applaud.

"Let it go, Chip," another man says.

Chip Gunther throws money on the table and storms out.

The Eagles watch him go. Franny stands next to me.

Their waitress says, "Don't you kids cause trouble in this place. Do you understand?"

I look at her, don't say anything.

"You do that again, you won't be welcome here."

No one wants any more pizza. We don't take the leftovers with us. We pay the bill, leave a tip for our waitress, who was nice, and walk out the door. It feels good to leave.

"Jeremiah, you were awesome," Terrell tells me.

"We were awesome," I say.

Chapter 36

I TELL WALT what happened.

"You took Gunther down, huh?"

"I felt a little like we were getting booed, so I did what you did."

Walt thinks about that.

"Do you think I did the wrong thing?"

"I think Gunther is the kind of man who might not let it go."

Chip Gunther calls El Grande and tells him that I don't know my place—he was just having a little fun, and he doesn't appreciate some smart-mouthed kid acting like he knows it all.

"What did you say to him?" I ask.

"I said I'd talk to you."

I explain about the turkey stuff and how I told him to please not call the team that again. "I was respectful."

"I believe that. And I would have done the same thing. It helps to be older when you deliver that kind of message. He'll spout off for a while, then it will be over."

Right now, Chip Gunther crosses the street whenever he sees me or Walt coming.

That's okay. We don't have to be friends. But now he knows something he didn't know before: he can't push me around, or the team.

❖ ❖ ❖

A priest and a nun from St. Peter's Middle School get off the bus first.

"They've got God on their side!" Logo wails.

Alvin points. "Look, we've got God, too." Rabbi Tova walks across the field and sits in our section.

El Grande goes over to meet the coaches as St. Peter's comes on the field. They have two girl players. Franny runs over to the girls. The nun marches forward. She's got a big whistle around her neck.

She shakes my hand hard. "Sister Claire."

"Jeremiah Lopper, ma'am. I'm Lutheran."

She slaps my shoulder. "That's close enough." Sister Claire blows her whistle.

The priest walks over. The St. Peter's team bows their heads. Logo waves to Rabbi Tova to get in on this.

The priest smiles at Rabbi Tova. "Rabbi . . . please . . ."

Our rabbi bows her head. "May the Source of All Life bless these players with wisdom and strength, swiftness and skill, patience and power. May their efforts on the field be for the good of all who enjoy this game with them, and may the winners show humility in victory and the losers good humor in defeat. And for the umpires—"

She's hitting all the bases.

"—blessed is the Source of Arcane Baseball Rules and those who tend them."

All the adults laugh.

Sky whispers, "What's *arcane* mean?"

I look it up. "Understood by only a few."

Sky sniffs. "No kidding."

Sister Claire blows her whistle. "Play ball!!!!!"

◆ ◆ ◆

There's a lot of arcane umpiring going on, but despite all that . . .

We are killing St. Peter's!

Franny hits two home runs and helps make a double

play at second when she throws to Donald, who makes the tag.

Sky's fastball is doing damage to their lineup, although the umpire calls two strikes as balls. That hurts us in the fourth inning.

Alvin is doing so much better in the outfield: he's running to catch the pop flies, and he's not running into his brothers in left and right field. He's also hitting well.

And Roy Nader, at shortstop, makes an impossible running catch for the third out in the sixth inning.

"There it is!" That's Rabbi Tova.

Roy comes off the field grinning, but Donald Mole has the biggest smile in Ohio as he high-fives Roy.

Mr. Hazard does an eagle groove. Donald's dad is cheering. A row of Hillcrest parents is doing the wave. Walt couldn't come. He had to work.

"Way to go!" I tell Roy.

"Great moves out there!" El Grande shouts.

Great is not how I'm feeling. I've just walked out to the pitcher's mound to tell Sky to throw his slider to the next two batters.

But I need to sit down. So I do, on the mound.

"You okay?" Sky asks.

"Yeah." I feel nauseous.

"You look sick, Jeremiah."

I try standing, which is harder than it looks when you're close to throwing up.

El Grande is by my side now, holding on to my arm.

"I just need to call Walt."

I sit down on the mound again.

I feel brain fog creeping in . . .

I think I hand someone my phone and tell them to call my father.

Chapter
37

"YOUR HEART RATE is quite low, Jeremiah." Dr. Dugan stands by my bed in the hospital. "I want to keep you overnight."

"I have to help the team."

She looks at Walt.

He gives me his eagle stare. "Jer, we're doing this."

"But—"

Walt shakes his head. "We're not taking any chances."

Both of them cross their arms and put their game faces on.

We're outnumbered, Alice.

Get strong.

◆ ◆ ◆

Beep beep, beep.

Beep beep, beep.

I've had three tests and now I'm supposed to sleep in a hospital bed in the land of never-ending white noise and beeping.

I'm not supposed to use my phone in this room because of the machines.

Walt took it home.

My phone!

I am disconnected from the world.

The team.

Franny.

I don't even know who won the game!

I close my eyes. Try to sleep. I have to go to the bathroom. The medicine they gave me does this. I have to call for a nurse to help me. I'm going to have to go soon. I hate this.

All this stuff about running one day . . .

Am I kidding myself? I mean, I'm attached to a machine—a machine named Marvin. I decided to name it that.

Beep beep, beep.

"Don't talk back to me, Marvin."

◆ ◆ ◆

Dr. Dugan is standing by my bed. It's early. "How are you?" she asks.

"Disconnected from the universe and other galaxies yet to be discovered," I mention.

"Well, you know what they say, Jeremiah: we all need to unplug a little, get some rest from the tyranny of electronics."

I look at the picture on the wall of a herd of wild horses running across a plain. None of those horses have heart problems. "This isn't restful."

"I hear that." She's reading my chart.

"Do you like my father?"

She looks up, half-smiling. "I like your father."

"On the chart of likes, how far up do you like him?"

She pushes her green reading glasses up on her nose and looks at me. "I'm not familiar with this chart."

"It goes from liking a person a little bit to liking them more than a little bit but not a lot, to liking them a whole lot."

"I can't answer that, Jeremiah."

I bet you could. You just don't want to.

"Do you have chest pain?"

"No."

"Shortness of breath? Dizziness?"

"No."

"Any other symptoms?"

"I want to unplug this machine, throw it out the window, and escape."

She smiles. "That's a good sign, actually. You can go home."

I push back the sheets.

"Let me disconnect you first. Your dad will be here pretty soon." She frees me from Marvin. "And, yes, Jeremiah, I like him a whole lot."

Chapter 38

WE WON!!!

That's the banner hanging across my porch.

I throw my hands in the air. We're going to the World Series! Okay, maybe not that, but it feels like we should.

I'm wearing Baxter, the heart monitor, again. I know it's recording this intense moment.

Franny runs over. "Three to two, Jeremiah!"

She shows me a picture of the team all together after the win. Everybody is there. Benny. The rabbi. Everyone except me.

"It got in the paper and everything," she adds.

"You knew this?" I ask Walt.

"I wanted you to see the sign."

The whole team signed it, plus Benny.

Franny hugs me. "We couldn't have won without

you, Jeremiah. Everyone said it. Are you coming to practice?"

I look at Walt, who shakes his head. "I guess I'll be there tomorrow."

"It'll be a few days," Walt explains.

Franny looks worried.

"I'm fine," I say, and head up the steps. That's when Benchant walks over, carrying his bat. He's never been to my house.

"You okay, Lopper?"

"Yeah."

He looks at the WE WON banner. "Can I talk to you?"

"Sure."

Walt and Franny stand there.

"Alone?" he says.

"Yeah, sure." We walk to the back, across the bridge. "Pull up a rock, Benchant."

He sits down. "I haven't liked you much, Lopper."

"I know."

"But that's not why I'm quitting the team."

Is he serious? "We just won."

"I know." He throws a pebble in the stream. It plops, makes no difference to the stream.

"Why, Bobby?"

"My dad said I need to do football so I can play in high school, since the Hornets . . . you know . . ."

"Is that what you want to do?"

"I think sometimes I'm better off in a game where I can shove people out of the way."

"Has your dad seen you play baseball?"

"Nah . . ."

That's hard.

"I'm done, Lopper. I wanted you to know."

"Well, whatever you do, you'll be good at it. I've been thinking about your strengths. They are many, Benchant."

He looks shocked. I don't think too many people say this to him. "They are?"

I nod. "Many."

"Many," he whispers.

"You've got the strength to be an awesome hitter."

"I do?"

"Plus you have the ability to drive a pitcher up-the-wall, into-the-stratosphere crazy."

A little smile forms on Benchant's face. "I like doing that."

"Jackie Robinson, the greatest ballplayer in history,

drove pitchers nuts. He stole bases. He threw their focus. You can do that, too, Bobby."

He's nodding.

"I'm sure you've thought about all the athletes who
were so good, they couldn't pick one sport. They gave
their all to baseball, then they gave what was left to
something else, like football. I'm sure you and your father have talked about this."

He grips his bat. "Not exactly."

"You hold that bat like it's part of you, Bobby."

Benchant stands up, swings it hard.

"That's power," I tell him.

"I could talk to my dad again."

I nod. "Mention the power of your swing."

"He already knows how irritating I am."

Benchant takes out his phone, walks to our fence. I
hear: "Listen, Dad. I've been thinking . . . No really! I want
to . . ." He walks farther away. He's deep in conversation.

The little stream keeps running like none of this
matters.

I throw a pebble in the water. Baseball matters.

Benchant walks back with his bat over his shoulder.
"I'll be at practice," he says.

I stand. "That's great, Bobby!"

"You're okay, Lopper. You're weird, but okay."

◆　◆　◆

SARBs are everywhere in my house. It's like a convention. You have to look where you're stepping. Jerwal tripped over a little blue one that likes to go fast. Walt and I had to put Jerwal's right hand back on.

I warn Franny about this before she comes over. Walt is working at the big table. "You," he says to the blue SARB, "get a time-out." He turns the SARB off and puts it on a shelf, lifeless.

Franny giggles as another SARB rolls by. "Hi," she says to it. The SARB doesn't respond. She and I are in the kitchen watching the eagle cam. Nature, unfortunately, is showing its dark side.

"This is usually inspiring to watch, Franny. I'm sorry about the predator."

We're watching new baby eagles in their nest as a hawk circles overhead.

"You said eagles were good parents, Jeremiah."

"They are. They might have gotten stuck in traffic."

"Isn't there someone to protect these babies?"

"Sometimes."

Franny stands up. "Why are we watching this?"

I'm trying to introduce the soaring concept, but—

"Are we going to watch the babies die?"

"No! A parent will come."

"You said they took turns guarding!"

"Well . . ."

"What's going to happen?" Franny shouts.

"They're eagles, Franny. They'll work it out!"

This isn't the best introduction to what I need to tell her, but I take the card out of my pocket. It has a picture of an eagle flying through a storm. It's the same one I gave to Yaff before I left St. Louis.

"In my opinion, and I've dealt with these things before, you're an eagle, Franny. You just don't know it."

She turns the card over. On the back is written one word:

SOAR

Franny looks at the eagle cam with the helpless babies. She looks back at the card.

This concept takes time to sink in.

She says, "Eagles molt, right?"

"Yes." This means they lose their feathers.

"And they're bald, right?"

"Some have white feathers on their heads; they just look bald."

We watch the circling hawk. The unfairness of the wild.

"I'm not sure I want to be associated with a bird who doesn't care about its babies!"

She gets up. A SARB rolls in front of her. "Excuse me," she says, and heads for the door.

Chapter

39

TO PLAY ONE more game—that's what we're all hoping for. And the latest we can play it is next week. After that the best teams battle it out for the championship. I need to know how much longer I have in Hillcrest.

Walt doesn't know. This isn't like him. "It could be much longer or shorter. I'm sorry. It's complicated, Jer."

No kidding!

I try to get him to zero in.

"Ten days, Walt? More?"

"I hope so."

I take out my phone, look up "What you can do in ten days."

- ◆ Get your kitchen remodeled (at least according to one kitchen contractor).

- ◆ Write a screenplay (probably not a good one).
- ◆ Lose five pounds.
- ◆ Visit China.

Note that "Save baseball" is not on this list.

◆ ◆ ◆

"Are we ever going to play another game?" Logo asks me.

I gulp. "Of course."

"Against who?" He looks around the park. "Squirrels?"

"I'll get back to you on that."

But even without an official game to get ready for, the Eagles are practicing anyway. Benny still comes to practice, but he's taking a new medicine and not talking as much. He is, however, out on the field, watching.

He stands near first base and watches Franny take grounders.

He stands in the outfield and watches as the Oxen catch flies.

He runs laps with us. He's a good runner—his problem is stopping. When he sees something interesting, like a butterfly or a bird, he stops.

Danny Lopez is coaching Benny on running. "Okay, Benny Man, this is for real. This is the answer you've been looking for." Benny looks confused. "'Cause it's about taking all your strength and getting it in your legs. Ready?"

Benny's not sure.

"Is that a yes or a no?" Danny asks him.

"A yes or a no," Benny says.

I'm leaving subtle reminders for Walt around the house.

> *Ten days left?*
> *It would be helpful to know something!*

> *Can you believe it's June already, Walt?*
> *It feels like we just got here. Nine days left?*

We are now at, possibly, eight days left and Walt has no information for me.

"When does the school year end, Jer?"

Every kid knows the answer to this. "June sixteenth. Two thirty-seven p.m."

Walt sighs. He deals with big concepts all day long. How hard can this be?

It would be helpful to know if we will play another game this season, but the adults in charge aren't saying anything about that either. I don't know what to tell the team this afternoon.

I know one thing—they're getting restless.

Terrell throws down his glove. "They're just going to let us practice and do nothing, Jeremiah!"

"We're a joke to them," Logo adds.

I see El Grande walking toward us. Maybe he's got news.

"Look!" Terrell points.

Across the street from the field, we see a group of guys moving toward us. They're so far away, we can't tell who they are.

Benny runs toward them.

I shout, "Not too far, Benny!"

He stops, looks, and runs back to us waving his hands. "Baseball men! Baseball men!"

What's he talking about?

But now we see them. Nine guys, big guys, with baseball gloves; some have bats over their shoulders.

I look at El Grande. He takes off his glasses, cleans them on his shirt, and puts them on again.

Terrell says, "It's the Hornets."

And they've got their game faces on. They walk right onto our field.

"You guys want to play?" the biggest guy asks us.

"You're Mac Rooney," Terrell whispers.

"Yeah," the big guy says. "You want to play . . . you know . . . a baseball game?"

We stand there.

"You need to practice, right?" another guy asks.

"And we haven't played for a while," another one adds.

"You'll kill us," Logo mentions.

Mac Rooney smiles. "Maybe." He's got that Baseball Is Life look as he studies the field.

El Grande shakes their hands. "We'd be honored, boys."

◆ ◆ ◆

In the first two innings, only Franny can get on base for the Eagles. She hits a line drive into the left-field gap and gets on second. In a middle school game, she would have been fast enough to make it to third. I'll tell you what—these guys are playing for real. But they're adding something more.

"You almost got a piece of that," their pitcher says to Handro. "Don't swing so hard."

At the top of the third inning, it's 8–0.

Guess who's the zero?

Mac Rooney says, "We need to mix it up." He talks to his team, and five of their players come onto the Eagles team. Joey Fitz, another Hornet, waves our other players over and says, "The girl can come with us."

Franny's face turns irritated purple as she marches over.

At the top of the sixth, it's 10–7. These are big numbers in baseball. El Grande tells Sky, "Make them go for the corners." That means the slider—Sky's big pitch. It looks like one thing coming at you and slides away before the batter can figure it out.

He strikes out Joey Fitz. Franny's up. She heads to the plate, snarling, "The girl can come with us."

She slices the first pitch, rams the second out of bounds. Benny is jumping up and down and clapping. "Franny's mad. Pow!"

The Hornets in the outfield move in closer like she can't hit far. That really steams her. The pitch comes, she cracks the ball. Mac Rooney watches it sail over him.

It's a home run!

Franny rounds the bases as Mac Rooney shakes his head.

I clap for her as she comes in—all the Eagles do. "Head in the game," I'm telling our guys. "Total focus. Tell me the numbers, Benny. Pitches?"

"Six seven." That's sixty-seven.

"Catches?"

"One two."

"Misses?"

"Six."

"Who do you think's going to win, Benny?"

"Franny!"

And, you know, it's too bad the town isn't out here to see us play. Because they'd see what this game can be and how people need it.

The Hornets are laughing—not all hyped up like they played at their stadium. They're cheering for one another, they're cheering for us.

El Grande stands there shaking his head, saying, "Well, I'll be."

I wish Mr. Hazard would come out dancing in his eagle outfit. I wish Dr. Selligman would watch and be amazed. I wish Chip Gunther could be here feeling totally guilty.

Benny is right. Franny's team wins. Franny goes three for three with a home run, a double, and a single.

Joey Fitz is looking around the field. "I used to play here."

"Me too," another Hornet says.

"You're welcome any time," El Grande tells them.

Joey grins. "We appreciate that, Coach."

Benny points to me. "He's Coach, too."

Joey shakes my hand. "Later, Coach Two."

"Yeah, later."

The Hornets walk off.

Pictures! I should have gotten pictures!

"Wait a minute!" I shout. And we do a group picture. Terrell lifts Benny up on his shoulders—normally, Benny wouldn't like this, but today, the miracle day, Benny raises his hands in the air and screeches like a baby eagle.

All the Eagles screech.

Click.

El Grande gets the best sports shot of the season.

"You guys are okay," Joey says.

"You guys, too."

◆　◆　◆

Word gets around town about the great game that everybody missed. El Grande sends the picture to the

Herald and it shows up on page one. Here's what I'm hoping: page one will be hard to ignore!

El Grande has a meeting with two coaches from the middle school league tomorrow. It's killing me that I can't be in that meeting. I think I could add a youthful perspective. I'm dying to know: "What are you going to tell them?"

"Well, that depends. First, I'm going to listen."

Chapter
40

I NEED SOMETHING else to focus on, and Donald
Mole still needs help. He's trying so hard; he's just . . .

"Stiff," says Danny. "I mean, he's got to move more
out there." We walk over to Donald, who is tying his
shoe. Danny says, "Mole. We gotta talk. We can make
you into a great baseball player." Donald looks up, surprised. "All you gotta do is one thing." Danny holds up
one finger. "One."

Mole waits to hear the thing.

Danny looks at me; he's moving around a little. "It's
about energy, Mole. It's about—"

"Hustle," I say.

"You leave it all on the field, every ounce you got."
Danny puts his hand on Donald's shoulder. "You gotta
practice it, not just on the field, but everywhere. Hustle."

"Hustle," Donald says flatly.

"Mole . . ." Danny makes a strange face. "We've gotta make a change. You can't half-hustle. You need a little sauce. Here's what we're going to do. Your name, Mole? In Spanish it's *mo-lay*. Same spelling. But it's not an animal that digs underground—no offense. It's the sauce of my country. It's got some bite, some heat. From this day forward, you're not Donald Mole. Okay? You're Donald *Mo-lay*. And you've got bite and heat."

This might be more than Donald Mole can handle, but suddenly his eyes light up. He stands a little straighter. "That's good," Danny tells him. "Walk around. Get used to it."

Donald tries this.

"Mo-lay, listen. You let this go down into your heart, now."

It's clear that Danny Lopez is going to be a great coach someday. Now I see El Grande walking toward us, smiling. He gives a thumbs-up. I think we've got a game!

The team gathers round. El Grande waits to speak. Then . . .

"In four days, we're playing the Millville Marlins."
What!

"I worked it out with their coach. This will be our

last game this season. League championship games start next week."

We didn't play enough games to qualify for that.

"The Marlins are a serious team," Terrell says.

"So are you."

El Grande looks toward the horizon. Actually, it's the parking lot, but you get the idea.

◆ ◆ ◆

I know this much: we need support! I walk into the school office. Dr. Selligman, the principal, is talking to the lady at the desk.

"The Eagles have one last game to play," I explain. "Will you come?"

The lady at the desk looks like she'd rather do almost anything than that. But Dr. Selligman grins wide.

"Jeremiah, I promise you I will bring people to that game and we will cheer so loud, you might be embarrassed."

Chapter 41

DR. SELLIGMAN IS good on both her promises.

1. She comes to our game and she brings people.
2. She totally embarrasses me.

Picture this: Dr. Selligman and her people sitting in the bleachers. So far, so good. Until . . .

Everyone in that group holds up little grinning eagle stuffies and makes them dance in the air. Not proper eagle stuffies with the power of Baby—miniature ones that look like chickens.

But the Millville Marlins have no one in their section holding up fish stuffies with long bills. They have nada for a mascot. They don't have a rabbi, either. And I can tell, they're nervous.

There's no prayer to begin this game, but Sky goes

over to where Rabbi Tova is sitting. He leans down and asks, "Would you . . . you know . . ."

She nods.

"Don't forget the umpires."

"Play ball!"

And it's like everything we've ever practiced—all the drills, all the fundamentals—never happened. The Eagles mess up again and again. I can't believe what I'm seeing!

Franny strikes out once. Sky's slider gets hit again and again. He walks two batters. The Oxen keep running into one another and can't catch a thing. At the bottom of the second inning, it's 4–0.

We're the zero.

"Just kill me now!" Danny shouts.

El Grande is saying, "It's okay. We got a little rusty. Remember the fundamentals: Eye on the ball. Don't swing at junk. Patience. Tire that pitcher out. Make him sorry you're at bat."

This pitcher is so glad we're at bat! I can feel the energy leaving us. What do I say to them?

And then the words of the coach-speech-I-want-to-give-someday come back to me. I put it together last year from inspirational coach sayings. I practiced it in front of the bathroom mirror with hand motions. I practiced it in front of Jerwal. It's the only speech I've got. I call a time-out and gather the team around me. I stand with my feet apart like coaches do, fold my arms across my chest, and drop my voice.

"Look, guys, I know you've worked hard. It hasn't been easy. But you've become—I've seen it—you've become a family. You look out for each other, and you don't sweat the small stuff." Everyone looks at Danny.

"Hey, come on!" he says. "I care!"

Back to me: "You haven't had a lot of chances, I know, but I also know you've got what it takes to win. You're Eagles, the kings—"

Franny glares at me.

"Sorry. The kings *and* queens of the sky. We're playing Marlins—big fish with long noses. You play your game, not theirs. Do you hear me? You give your best to this team and to this game we all love." I add, "This is your time."

Danny looks like he might start crying. This is the kind of emotion a coach hopes for. Too bad he can't play.

"This is your win," I tell them. "Now get out there and take it."

I step back. They look at one another and do the

eagle screech. They run on the field, except for Franny. "Fry those fish!" Danny shouts after them.

Franny looks at me. "I've heard some of that before, Jeremiah."

"I adapted it. Okay?"

She runs to first base. I have to sit down and stay sitting. But my Eagles keep the Marlins from scoring in the third inning. I'm clapping. "All right now!"

Fourth inning—we get one run when Franny homers on a three-two pitch.

"That's the way Eagles play!"

The Marlins get a run, too.

It's 5–1 heading into the fifth.

We hold the line, but so do the fish.

It's the sixth inning—Rabbi Tova stands and shouts, "Be aggressive!"

Now everyone in our section is standing. Every eagle stuffy is raised. Hillcrest parents are cheering. I look at Walt, who has one arm in the air and the other one around Dr. Dugan.

Everyone is shouting, "Eagles, Eagles!"

Mr. Hazard stands with his eagle arms in the air.

Hargie Cantwell's dad locks arms with four Hornets players and they holler, "Go Eagles!"

Yes!

"Eagles! Eagles!"

And then it really hits me. If we lose, we let everyone down.

And then we'll really seem like—

Wait a minute! That's not right!

I holler, "Eagles, remember who you are! Play your game!"

The Oxen raise their gloves.

Jupiter's pitching now. He throws a two-two slider and strikes the batter out.

Aiden catches a fly ball, and his brother lets him do it.

Franny fields a grounder and gets the third out at first base.

The cheers are rocking this place.

Our turn at bat.

"You already know how to connect with the ball," El Grande tells them. "Don't tell yourself you don't. Hit the ball. Get on base."

Danny is standing on the bench, waving his arm that doesn't have a cast. "We can do it! We can do it!"

Jupiter's up, drags a bunt, and gets on first!

Yes!

That surprises the Marlins pitcher. He throws balls after that. Benchant moves to first on a walk. Two men on.

Terrell takes a full count, then hits a grounder to the shortstop. Jupiter is out at third, but Terrell is safe on first. Benchant is on second.

One out, people. Only one out!

"Eagles! Eagles!"

I can tell the noise is getting to Benny. He's covering his ears and rocking. I smile at him. *Hold on, Benny.* I motion for him to come sit with me. He does. "Good game," I say.

That's when Benchant makes a tear to third base and steals it!

I'm not kidding!

He's teasing the pitcher a little, too—jumping half on, half off the base. I hope his dad is here.

Okay, okay, okay . . .

Aiden walks past us to take his turn at bat.

"No," Benny says to me. He points at Donald, sitting on the bench.

"What do you mean?"

"Him."

"Donald?"

Benny nods.

"Benny, why?"

He can't tell me, but I can see in his eyes he knows something. And I've read about these things, when a coach has to make a hard decision on the spot. El Grande's been listening. He nods and says, "Aiden, come back. We've got a substitution. Donald. You're up."

Donald looks surprised, the team looks surprised, but Benny smiles. Danny hollers, "Olé, Mol-ay!"

Donald takes a couple of swings, adjusts his batting helmet, crouches to hit. On the first pitch, he slaps one deep into center field for a double!

I stand up. "Yes!"

Benchant scores easily. Terrell tears around the bases and slides into home under a high throw to the catcher.

"Safe!" the umpire shouts.

We are now, people, 5–3! With one out! Danny's dancing.

"Talk to me, Benny!" I can see he can hardly hear with the noise. He's covering his ears.

"Eagles! Eagles!"

Franny's up.

Benny studies her. "Pow," he says.

"Yeah, we want that, Benny!"

He looks at me. "Franny mad!"

"No, she's not mad."

Franny puts her batting helmet on.

Wait a minute. Benny is pointing at Franny. "Franny mad!"

I look at him. "You mean . . . Franny hits better when she's mad?"

She does, all right. But who's going to get her mad?

Benny stares at me.

Okay, okay. I raise my hand, make the time-out sign, and walk to her.

I've got one-tenth of a second to say something that will totally enrage her.

She looks at me. "What is it?"

Here goes. "Don't play like a girl."

Her eyes blaze. Now her face has splotches, which is very good. She screams, "Step away, Jeremiah, and let me hit the ball!"

Happy to do that. I go back to my seat. Benny is smiling. "Franny mad!"

She's mad, all right. She might never talk to me again.

The first pitch is junk. She waits. The second is right down the middle, and the crack of her bat is pure power. Franny Engers hits it like a girl, and that ball is outta here! Donald Mole scores. Franny runs the bases, happy but furious.

I go up to Franny. "Good one! That was awesome!"

"Do not talk to me, Jeremiah! Go somewhere far away!"

"I did it on purpose! I just wanted you to use all your—"

"Far away," she says.

This is what it means to take one for the team.

The scoreboard reads: 5–5.

We've got to push ahead. No one is sitting.

Handro's up at bat. He hasn't looked sharp today; he's been swinging at everything.

"Take your time, son," El Grande tells him.

It's a full count; then he gets hit by a pitch. The umpire calls, "Take your base," and he trots to first, rubbing his shoulder. El Grande sends me to coach first base. Logo's up. He hasn't had a hit yet.

I tell Handro, "This guy's a right-handed pitcher. His back's to first base. Are you getting this?"

Handro says, "Yeah." He takes a big lead off the base. The second pitch bounces in the dirt, Handro tears to second, and he's safe!

Lightning shoots across this place as Logo steps back into the batter's box, but he strikes out.

We didn't need that. "Keep that energy!" I shout.

Alvin is up. He gets three balls, then connects with a real pitch and hits it over the first baseman's head. It rolls slowly down the line, and Handro dashes to third. I shout, "Go home!" He makes a tear for it.

"Safe!" the umpire shouts.

6–5.

We are the six!

"Eagles! Eagles!"

Rabbi Tova screams, "That's the way!"

The Marlins don't like that call; their coach makes a protest.

Please. He was safe by a mile.

A Marlin parent starts screaming at the umpire. The Marlins change pitchers as the screaming parent storms off. It takes time for their new pitcher to warm up. We've got to keep the momentum going.

"Keep it running in your head," El Grande says.

It's too much for Benny, who runs to his mom and

buries his head in her arms. *You did so good for the team, Benny!*

The new Marlins pitcher throws three fastballs in a row and strikes Alex out. He walks away from the plate, head down.

The final inning. If we can hang on to the lead, we win, but anything can happen, and does in baseball. We take the field. Donald has replaced Aiden in right field. Jupiter Jetts runs onto the mound. He strikes two Marlins out in a row. Then a high fastball—the batter swings and hits a long fly ball to deep right field. This is bad—that's at least a double!

Alvin's too far away in center to reach it. Donald scrambles to get underneath it.

And, yes, there are miracles.

Oh, yes, there are!

Mole makes a two-handed catch, trips, and falls— but he never lets go of the ball.

We win!

Danny runs out to the field.

Mr. Hazard swoops in a circle. Benny runs under the stands! The Eagles run everywhere.

I look to Walt, who is hugging Dr. Dugan as eagle stuffies dance.

El Grande slaps me on the shoulder, and we head to the field to shake the Marlins' hands and say "Good game."

"You guys were awesome," their second baseman says.

"You guys, too."

Benny is still under the stands, hugging his knees and rocking. His mother goes to get him. Benny is waving his arms as he talks to her. He's wearing his glove.

The Marlins clear the field. Then Mrs. Lewis takes Benny by the hand and walks him over to us.

"Benny wants to ask you something," she says. Benny shakes his head and pushes his mom forward. "I guess Benny wants me to ask you." She looks down at him, smiling. "Benny would like to play catch with the team."

Terrell grabs the baseball—"Come on, big man"— and runs out to the field with Donald, Benchant, and Roy. The Oxen race after them, and Logo and Handro follow with Sky and Jupiter. Franny shouts, "Close in, guys!" The Eagles form a circle.

"Come on, Benny!"

Benny takes time to adjust his glove. He takes it off, puts it back on. Then he smiles and runs out to the field with his head down and gets close to Franny.

"Big throw, Benny." Terrell tosses an easy one at Benny, who drops it. "That's okay. Throw it back."

Benny throws it not close to anyone. The Oxen run to get it, jabbing one another along the way.

Alvin gets close and plops the ball into Benny's glove. Benny laughs as he puts his hand over it and twirls around like it's the best day of his life.

Anyone want to tell me that baseball doesn't matter?

Chapter
42

I DIDN'T THINK any more could be packed into this week, but then . . .

The Magellan Group makes a unanimous decision (Walt is the only voting member) to move its corporate headquarters from St. Louis to Hillcrest, Ohio.

This accomplishes two things.

1. I get to go to seventh grade and beyond in this town and continue to coach the Eagles.
2. Walt and Dr. Dugan can get married.

I know. The marriage part seems a little fast to me, too, and I mentioned this to Walt.

"It is fast, Jer. But when you know, you know."

It seems fast to Yaff back in St. Louis, too, who doesn't think it's a good idea.

"Walt says I can visit and you can come here."

"It won't be the same, Eagle Man."

I know. Change is like that.

It also seems fast to Jerwal, who has always had the run of the house except for the bathroom. Dr. Dugan is threatening to put up a sign:

ABSOLUTELY NO ROBOTS IN THE BEDROOM

I talk to Jerwal, two SARBs, and the newest baby robot, a little brown one so small, it can fit in a pocket. I call it Son of SARB. "I think it's limiting, you guys. We're going to get a new house, and I wish you could have the run of it, but it's out of my hands. It's not that she doesn't care, believe me . . ."

I mention to Dr. Dugan that we could program the robots to go down the aisle of the church—before the bride, of course. She says no to that one, too.

The wedding is in six weeks. Aunt Charity is coming. I tell her, "You're not going to believe how mature I am." She asks when the last time we cleaned the refrigerator was. I let Walt answer that one.

Walt and Sarah (I'm calling her that now) are looking for a new place to buy. I mention it's important for us to live within walking distance of Franny's house. I also ask if they are planning on having other children.

"I might be enough for any couple," I warn them.

There's a lot that's up in the air.

Sarah might not be fully into life with robots, but she totally gets eagles. She and I are watching the eagle cam streaming live from the Nature Conservancy. The father eagle is showing the babies how to fly. One little bird has just flown to another branch. We applaud. The other wants to stay in the nest.

"They don't know they're eagles yet, Sarah. They have to learn what they can do."

"I see that, Jeremiah." She's focused on the baby in the nest. "Come on, baby. You can do it."

"The mother died tragically, but the father didn't give up."

The father eagle flies close to the nest to give the baby the general idea. He flutters a little, as the baby takes a deep eagle breath, jumps off, and flaps like crazy. It just makes it to the other branch.

"Yay!" we shout.

I can tell that Sarah is impressed by this eagle. She says, "Jeremiah, I want to help you fly as long and as far as you can."

This is a very positive sign. Some new mothers just march ahead and don't want input.

I do have one big worry, and I mention it at dinner.

"Sarah, will they still let you take my insurance?"

"Actually, you'll be getting another doctor. It's best that way. But I'll keep watch."

I count. "That will be my fifth cardiologist!"

"See how lucky you are? Some kids don't even have one."

◆ ◆ ◆

Walt is so happy, it's almost weird. He's cleaning the house and barbecuing more. He's throwing out his shirts that have stains on them.

"Don't change too much," I warn him.

"We're all going to change a little after the wedding, Jer. It takes time to get the lineup right. You know this."

I know this. We're having a series of pre-family meetings to discuss realities. Sarah brings her dachshund Hillary along. Hillary is not a team player. She barks constantly at Jerwal, which sends him into a corner. Once she pees on a SARB, who shuts right down.

"She never does this!" Sarah shouts. It's going to

take a lot of visits for Hillary and the robots to be able to deal with each other.

Another Big Issue is baseball—Sarah is a Red Sox fan, being from Boston, and doesn't root for other teams. We are Reds, Cardinals, Cubs, and Yankees fans. Actually, there has yet to be a baseball game played that I know of where I couldn't find a team to root for. I'm concerned that the playoffs might be difficult.

I make the mistake of walking into the kitchen when Walt and Sarah are kissing. I leave fast. Another time they were kissing in the hall. Later, I will mention the importance of No Kissing Zones in the house, but not tonight.

Tonight I bring out Baby and tell the story.

Sarah is quiet as I do. She is studying Baby the way she looks at an X-ray. "Do you know what I see, Jeremiah?"

"What?"

"First, an eagle stuffy shows great distinction— about you and who was taking care of you before. And second, no one remembers their lives when they were a baby. No one. We piece that part together by what others tell us. So I'm inclined to think that those first nine months for you are symbolized by this eagle." She picks Baby up, smiling. "What a gift."

I'm quiet now. I hadn't thought of it telling the story of my life before Walt.

"I think," Sarah says, "we carry love with us, even if we don't remember the people who loved us."

I agree with that.

Then she tells me, "I was adopted, too."

I can't believe this. "You were?"

"I was a baby. Three months old. My birth mother was a fifteen-year-old girl who lived in Georgia. I tried to find her when I was older, but she died before she turned eighteen. An overdose. I don't know anything about my biological father."

Walt's phone buzzes. He smiles at us and quietly leaves the table.

Sarah rubs Hillary's head. "My adopted parents always told me that I grew in their hearts. I loved that. It might be why I became a cardiologist."

I laugh, because it's all kind of perfect. That is, until Hillary pees on a SARB again.

"Bad dog!" Sarah scoops Hillary up. "She never does this."

She's done it twice now—I think she likes it.

Sarah takes Hillary out back; I sit at the table thinking about hearts.

You can look at one in a laboratory all covered with blood and wonder, how can something so ugly have so much power?

You can have yours beaten up by all kinds of things and wonder if you'll ever feel right again.

You can have a weak one and wonder if it can ever be fixed.

You can get a new one, not just by a transplant, but by people around you giving you love and courage.

Uncle Jack, who was very good at cards, always told me, "It's not the hand you're dealt that matters—it's the way you play it."

Uncle Jack played his hand strong until the end. I wish he could have known Sarah.

I put my hand over my heart.

Alice, we're getting a new mother . . . with a seriously big heart.

But she is still my doctor, and I need a few tests, which makes everything difficult.

Chapter 43

THE MVP (Most Valuable Player) Award dinner is being held, possibly for the first time in the history of sports, in a hospital cafeteria.

Two days ago my heart started beating too fast and my blood pressure went up. I told Sarah, "I'm really fine." She said, "I'd like you to be finer than this."

By "this" she meant a little nauseated, just a little; a little tired; a little pale.

"I'm naturally pale," I mentioned.

Walt drove me to the hospital with Sarah. I figured I was staying overnight. Sarah waved her hand in the ER and things happened fast.

"How are you feeling?"

Everyone asked me this. The guy drawing blood. The woman giving me an echocardiogram. The guy who brought me Jell-O.

"I don't do Jell-O," I told him.

Being in the hospital meant I couldn't be more involved in helping choose the MVP for the season. I know that El Grande won't choose Franny because she's his granddaughter, but she should be considered. I gave him my short list for who should win.

Franny
Terrell
Sky

We ordered a serious trophy with an eagle on the top. Not a cartoon eagle, either—a real one that glares at you: *Don't mess with me.*

Walt slept in a chair by my bed all night. He's gotten very good at sleeping in hospital chairs.

I'm tired. Now my blood pressure is too low again.

You'd think winning big in front of everybody would have a positive effect.

Alice, winning is good for the heart.

Just even out. Got that?

Sarah is in her white coat, checking the machines around my bed. I've got an IV in my arm.

"I don't have to have the IV at the dinner, right?"

"Correct. I'm taking it out now."

Sarah takes the needle out so easily, it hardly hurts.

"I'm also not wearing the hospital gown to dinner." The one I'm wearing has little bears on it—a downside of being in pediatrics.

"I don't know, Jeremiah. Think of the photo ops."

"You and Walt are perfect together."

She beams. "I know . . . and you can get dressed now. Your dad's waiting for you downstairs."

I go into the bathroom that smells like antiseptic, put on my one pair of good pants and a white shirt.

"How do you feel?" she asks.

I put my arms out like wings. "Fantastic."

"You look very nice. Shall we?"

Sarah and I head downstairs to the cafeteria. I'm glad I don't have to miss the awards dinner, but I hate it when people make a fuss because of me.

◆ ◆ ◆

When I see the trophy, I almost have a heart attack. First, it's by the Jell-O section in the hospital cafeteria. I would like to make this clear:

There is no Jell-O in baseball!

Worse than that—the eagle on the trophy is not the one I ordered. I ordered a gold eagle—this eagle is blue! Blue is a complicated color for me, because when my old heart was failing, my skin was a little blue. Gold is a non—medical emergency color.

I stare at the blue eagle.

El Grande walks up. "They were out of gold eagles."

How is that possible?

But in life, I've learned you have to adjust.

Walt comes over, and we sit at the head table with Franny, El Grande, Dr. Selligman, and Mr. Hazard, who has less of a personality when he's not the official Hillcrest Eagle.

Benny's mom and dad are telling him everything that's going to happen so he doesn't get surprised, but Benny doesn't want to sit at the table. He carries his chair over to the wall and sits there.

El Grande gets up, walks to the podium, and says to the group, "In honor of these dinners, we've found a good source of rubber chicken for your enjoyment. And if anybody has trouble digesting, I guess we're in the right place to take care of that."

People laugh.

He grins. "How do I talk about this crazy season? How do we bring it to a close? I . . . well . . . I don't think we do. I think it's our launching pad for the new day. I've been coaching baseball on and off for a few decades now, but I learned something with this team of Eagles that I'd not understood before.

"I'd always taken baseball for granted. I never thought it wouldn't be here for me. I'm not saying we didn't need to stop and reevaluate after all that happened in Hillcrest—we did. But baseball is worth fighting for. Not just because it's a game, but because of what it teaches you, what you become if you play it right. I've never been prouder of a team than you Eagles. I've never seen better teamwork in such a short time. And, Jeremiah—if you don't end up managing a major league ball club, then something will have gone terribly wrong in the world."

"Here here," Mr. Hazard says.

I grin and look at Walt as people applaud.

El Grande leans into the microphone. "Jeremiah, I have something for you tonight. Because, son, you've got it all, and you didn't hold any of it back from me or from this team. Jeremiah Lopper, I am so pleased to announce that you are the recipient of the MVP Award."

There's a burst of applause.

I just stare at El Grande.

What's he talking about? I didn't play!

Walt slaps my shoulder.

I'm not sure what to do.

El Grande chuckles and points at me. "And I know that mind of yours is going full tilt, saying, 'What are you doing, old man? I didn't play!' Isn't that right, Jeremiah?"

I nod and look down.

"Well, I found this definition: a player is a person who takes part in a sport or a game. And, son, you took your part, and because you did, we're all here. You coached everyone on this team, including me. So come on up and get this beast of a trophy."

Franny walks over in a pretty blue dress holding the trophy with the blue eagle.

Honestly, I don't know if I can go up there, because I don't want to cry.

But I can't say I don't want it.

I absolutely do!

So I walk up, tough, with eagle focus. No way do eagles cry.

El Grande slaps me on the back. "We'll have your name put on later."

Everybody stands up to clap for me, which has

never happened, and when you're trying not to cry, it's best to look at the weirdest thing in the room. So I focus on the Oxen doing the wave, standing on their chairs, carrot curls sticking out of their nostrils.

I look at Benny, who is sitting in his chair by the wall, hugging himself, but smiling big at me.

Franny hands me the trophy. It's heavy, but not so heavy that I can't lift it high. She's not mad at me anymore.

"Congratulations. You totally deserve this."

"I'm not sure I do, but I'm not giving it back."

The people who work in the cafeteria are shouting, "Yeah, man! Yeah!" I wave.

Doctors in white coats are clapping. I nod to them, because doctors kept me alive for this moment.

I walk back to my table and sit down. Walt's eyes are red—if he starts crying, I'm finished. Sarah is cheering. I will probably hug the trophy when I get home, but not now. People are still applauding even though it's time to stop. El Grande says something else, but honestly I don't hear it.

I should be listening, but I feel something new and strong breaking through me. And I just know that in years to come, when they ask me, *What was the thing that turned your heart around? What healed it?* . . .

I'll say, *It was baseball that did it.*

Every hit.

Every miss.

Every person.

Isn't that right, Alice?

Epilogue

- Coach Perkins will stand trial for second-degree murder in Cincinnati.
- Hillcrest Middle School is now the "Home of the Eagles: Changing for the better, learning how to soar."
- Sarah said I gave the Eagles wings!
- Walt dropped the ring at the wedding. It went rolling under a pew, but Franny, a great fielder, scooped it up and tossed it to me. I handed it to Walt. Double play.

The End . . .
Or maybe it's The Beginning.

Acknowledgments

With thanks to the team of good people who generously shared
their wisdom and experience:

- Dr. Jean Brown, Rhode Island College
- Dr. Sarita Dhuper, pediatric cardiologist
- Natima Harry, amazing heart transplant patient
- Dr. Laura Bruno, pediatrician
- Dr. Bruce Yaffe, internist
- Dr. Jeffrey Thompson, family medicine
- Phil Kluger
- Teresa LaMaster
- Mary Lester
- Twylah King, teacher of "special kids" at Nuttal Middle School
- Cindy Edwards
- Rabbi Toba Spitzer of Congregation Dorshei Tzedek, and
  author of the baseball prayer in Chapter 36
- Regina Hayes, my superb editor
- Janet Pascal and her copyediting team: Kate Hurley and
  Ryan Sullivan
- Gerard Mancini, associate publisher
- Nancy Brennan, designer
- Danielle Calotta, jacket designer
- Plus JoAnn, Laura, Rita, Karen, Tim, Mickey, Kally,
  Dorothea, and Chris

And special thanks to Hope Taft, who years ago gave this story
wings when she took me to the Crane Creek Wildlife Research
Center in Oak Harbor, Ohio, to see the eagles nesting.

KEEP READING FOR A TEASER OF
Almost Home

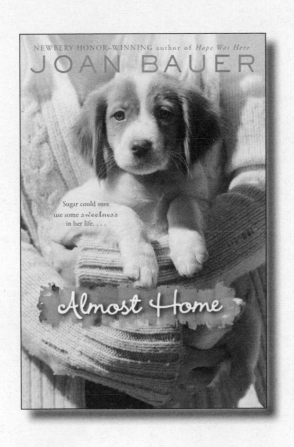

1

MR. BENNETT WALKED into room 212 carrying a plastic bag. He smoothed his sweatshirt that read DEATH TO STEREOTYPES, tucked Claus his rubber chicken under his arm, raised one eyebrow, and jumped on his desk. He opened the bag, lifted a loaf of bread into the air and shouted, "Sell it to me."

He threw the bread on the desk.

Peyton Crawler let his eyes go back into his head like he'd been dead for years. Harper Wilhelm hollered, "It's good for you."

Everyone in sixth-grade English groaned. Mr. Bennett shook his head. "It has to be more than that."

"You're hungry," Katie Nesbitt said.

Mr. B shrugged.

I see where he's going. I raised my hand. "Do you like toast?"

Peyton Crawler smirked. "That's stupid."

Go back to being dead, Peyton.

"As a matter of fact," Mr. B announced, "I love toast."

I pressed in. "With butter and jam?"

He pulled down his orange wool hat and grinned. "Strawberry jam."

I had what I needed. I ran up and grabbed the bread. "Then I can tell you, that this bread"—I looked at the label—"Aunt Fanny's Homemade Honey Bread, makes *the* best toast in the universe."

Mr. Bennett jumped off the desk and looked at the price. "It's expensive."

"It costs more because it's better," I told him. "And you can freeze half of it, and only use it when you want toast. It'll make you so happy, you won't be able to stand it."

He walked to the huge B that hung on the wall behind his desk—the Great B, he called it. "Sold." He slammed Claus on the desk (rubber chickens don't mind). "Why did she sell me?"

Kids looked at each other, clueless. Mr. B twirled Claus in the air. "These are golden lessons from my checkered career in advertising. *Think*. What did Sugar do?" Mr. Bennett was in advertising for fifteen years and made real decent money, but he gave it all up to teach sixth grade.

Katie raised her hand. "She had to learn about you before she could sell you the bread."

"That's right. She persuaded me. She formed an argument to convince me." He stood in front of the smaller B on the wall—the not-so-great B. "So, when you are trying to sell someone something—an idea, a loaf of bread, whatever—find out what the person is about."

Mr. Bennett held up an ad with a picture of a cool-looking singer standing by a piano. "What's wrong with this picture?" he asked us.

Simon said, "There's nothing wrong with it."

"Look closer," Mr. Bennett suggested.

Carrie said, "I love her dress."

Mr. Bennett looked at the ad. "Nice dress."

I said, "She's holding a cigarette in her left hand. You don't see it at first."

Mr. Bennett nodded. "And why is that?"

"They're trying to show that smoking is cool," Carrie said.

"They're trying to manipulate you," Mr. Bennett said. "Your mind takes in the photo—you don't notice the cigarette at first, if ever, but it's there."

"They want us to smoke," I said.

"That's right."

And my mind went to Mr. Leeland, my father, who looked so good in so many ways, being handsome and funny and seeming to love life, but in his left hand there was always a losing hand.

"Persuasion is an art. It can be misused or it can be powerful. Tonight, I want all of you, including the dead among us"—Mr. B threw Claus into Peyton's lap—"to write a stirring paragraph on one way you have seen persuasion misused—an advertising campaign, something on the Internet, something in your life. Specifics are found on thegreatbknowsall.com."

I wondered if I should write about Mr. Leeland and how he always persuaded Reba to believe he was going to come through for us.

"I will read the best three out loud in class, so work excessively hard on this."

I wouldn't want anything about Mr. Leeland read out loud.

Harper Wilhelm was giving me her evil eye like she knew all my secrets. I smiled and walked past her. Reba says it's good to smile around people who don't like you—it makes you stronger. I beamed a big one in Harper's direction; she looked disgusted and left the room. I walked up to Mr. B. He was exactly my height—five feet four inches. His ski cap had dogs on it.

"Mr. B, I've got something real personal I want to write about, but I wouldn't want the class to hear it."

He adjusted his hat. "Well, make it so good, it will kill me not to read it out loud."

I grinned. "I'll try." I stood there because I didn't want to go home. I wished I could tell him all that was happening at my house. "I'm not sure how to start writing about it."

He leaned Claus against his coffee mug. "Writing about personal things isn't easy, Sugar. Try breaking it up into small, manageable pieces."

Small and manageable was not what my life was like.

He looked at me. "Are you okay?"

That depends on how you define okay.

x   x   x

I walked home with Meesha Moy, my best friend. Her life wasn't small and manageable either. Even when we were a block from her house, we could hear the sound of bad accordion music carried on the wind. Meesha stopped walking and shook her head. Two months ago, her family had to rent out her room to Mr. Denton who played, or tried to play, the accordion. Meesha had to sleep on the couch in the TV room. Her dad got sick and the bills were killing them. We had a lot in common, except that Meesha's dad couldn't work because he was sick. Mr. Leeland didn't work because he was a gambler.

We haven't had to rent out a room . . . yet.

The bad accordion music got louder; a dog started howling. Meesha looked like she could start howling, too, but Reba taught me to be grateful no matter what. I looked up at the blue sky. "It's a pretty day, huh?"

Meesha glared at me. "If it was raining, he wouldn't be practicing on the porch."

I nodded and headed down Pleasant Street, my street, working hard at my gratitude. Reba was always telling me, "You take the *G-R* out of gratitude and you've got attitude."

Only once did I mention that attitude's got three *T*'s, not two.

"I'm teaching you enduring concepts for living," she snapped. "Not spelling."

Chester, our postman, was pushing his cart down the street. My grandpa, King Cole, was a mailman until the day he died. "Mail tells a story," he always told me. "A good mail carrier knows what's going on in every house on his route. They know who's paying their bills on time, they know who's late."

Chester looked at me with sympathy and handed me a stack of envelopes all marked URGENT. I hate that word. Only one was addressed to me, or halfway at any rate. It had curlicue writing.

Sugar Booger Cole
14 Pleasant St.
Round Lake, MO

I sighed. Sugar isn't the easiest name to be slapped with, I'll tell you. I was supposed to get named Susannah. I was supposed to get born in a hospital, too, but my whole life started as one big surprise when I got born in the back of a Chevy in the parking lot of the Sugar Shack in Baton Rouge in a rainstorm so bad, my parents couldn't make it to the hospital. When I popped out and Reba saw the Sugar Shack sign, she felt it was a sign from God; right then I got my name. At least God told her to stop at Sugar. Sugar Shack Cole would have been a chore to live with. As for Mr. Leeland, he got the thrill of helping me get born, and believe me, he hasn't done squat to help since then.

But I was grateful. As soon as I could write, I sent a note to the Chevrolet company in Detroit, Michigan, and thanked them for making such good backseats that a baby could get born and be okay. That company cared so much, they wrote me back and said that although many babies had been born in Chevrolet backseats over the years, I was the first one they knew of named Sugar.

Reba says part of why I'm on this earth is to bring a little sweetness into people's lives. "And sweet doesn't mean stupid," she says. "Sweet doesn't mean weak. I'm not talking kittens wearing sun hats either. I'm talking kindness. You go out there, Sugar Mae Cole, and show 'em what it means to be sweet."

I threw the Sugar Booger envelope into the garbage and walked up the path to our house. The yellow paint was cracked and our porch needed repair, but we had hanging flowerpots that made up for some of that. Reba was sitting on the porch in a white chair with her pink phone to her ear, clutching the little silver bell on the necklace Mr. Leeland had given her last year right before she kicked him out for the umpteenth time. Mr. Leeland got it in Atlanta and called it her southern bell. Reba's big desire is to be a fine Southern belle, which is kind of like being a lady on steroids.

When Reba clutched that bell, it meant she was ready to pop off and working hard to find her graces.

"Why yes," she said into her pink phone, "yes, I know, and I'm terribly sorry we're late again." Her voice went deep Southern now, pouring the words out like hot butterscotch melting vanilla ice cream. "But I'm struggling as it is to pay the rent. Surely, sir, you understand that I can't manage the late fee." Reba clung to that bell like it was a lifesaver. She closed her eyes. "Why, yes, I hope we will be able to resolve this soon as well. You have a nice day now." She flipped her phone shut and shouted, "Honking, skinflint moron! If his brains were dynamite, he couldn't blow his nose!"

I wanted to know more about the late fee, but I decided not to ask. King Cole always told me, "If you've got a good, fair question and you ask it at the wrong time, what do you get?"

Answer: "In trouble."

I kissed Reba on the head and went inside to start my paragraph on bad persuasion.

It's always good when homework can help you manage a part of your life.

2

THERE ARE PEOPLE *in our lives we cannot*
 trust.
One of those people in my life is my father.
Is there Gorilla Glue for fathers, I wonder?
Duct tape to keep one together?
I remember so much and wish I didn't.
All the fights about him borrowing money and
 never paying it back.
All the times he'd play cards with me for money.
I was little, but he always won.
There was a strange look in his eyes when that
 happened.
Sometimes he'd disappear and not come back for
 the longest time.
He had the gift of persuasion.
His voice sounded like he meant every word,
His eyes would fill with love,

And it was hard to believe he didn't mean what
    he said,
But he didn't.
I've learned a lot having a father like this.
One of the big lessons is that you learn about
    people
Not just by the words they say, or the promises
    they make,
But by what they do.
I want to be the kind of person who does what I
    say I'll do.
I want people to know they can trust me.

Mr. B said to write a paragraph, but the words of this poem poured out of me from some secret place. He was going to have to adjust.

There were probably lots of poems to write about my father.

My grandma, Mr. Leeland's mother, used to say, "You be respectful of your father, Sugar, for he's been through harder times than you know."

I didn't know what those hard times were, other than all the times he lost money gambling. I asked King Cole how you respect someone you don't trust.

"Now, that's one the great minds have been wrestling with for ages. It's not the easiest thing to do. They're all agreed on that."

"Did they come up with an answer a kid can understand?"

"It just so happens they did. Everyone alive has good parts and bad parts to them. Some people work hard to develop the good parts, and others work hard on the bad. I think we can respect a person's potential—what they could be—but we don't have to like it if they're acting the wrong way. Do you know what I mean?"

"Like they've got good things inside they don't know how to get at?"

"That's right—they're in a locked drawer."

"And they can't find the key."

He grinned and wrote that down in his notebook. "That's good truth, isn't it? And I'm giving you full credit for this one." He wrote some more. "'This concept was inspired by Sugar Mae Cole, one of the great minds of our time.'"

I laughed. "I am not."

"It's my book. I say what I believe."